They of the West

Dani Finn

Dragonheart Press

Content warnings

This book is appropriate for older young adult and adult audiences; content warnings include hunting/butchery, smoking, drinking, cursing, and brief references to sexual topics.

Copyright © 2024 by Dani Finn

Cover art © 2024 by Dani Finn, based on an original photograph

All rights reserved.

No portion of this book may be reproduced in any form without written permission from the publisher or author, except as permitted by U.S. copyright law.

1

Dralen ran his fingers absently through the blood-spotted tracks in the sand, which had told him nothing new. The nildeer was injured but still moving at a steady trot, despite the unseasonable heat in the wake of the dragon winds. His sling bullet had missed by an inch and hit it on the nose instead of between the eyes, and it had fled, disoriented but faster than he'd hoped. If it kept up like this, he'd lose it in the canyons before dark.

He should turn back. He had three more slickback traps to check, and he had a good feeling about the one on the ledge above the little creek. But the thought of letting the nildeer hobble into the canyons to die didn't sit right with him. If the wolves didn't get it, the Logans surely would, ripping it apart as its squeals of terror echoed off the indifferent stone walls, then devouring it in their midnight feasts.

Dralen shivered.

The sun was two fingers above Fishback Ridge, so he figured he could follow the nildeer for another hour before he had to head back at a fast run. The Logans were said to come out of the canyons at the same time as the bats. When the sun dipped below the ridge, nildeer or no, he was on his way home.

He picked up his pace, guessing the direction of the nildeer whenever he saw no tracks or blood. He found an indentation where it had rested, along with more blood. As he crested the next rise, he saw it lying in the grass, chest heaving slowly. He curled his hand into a fist, but his relief lasted only a moment as he saw the sun disappearing behind Fishback Ridge and realized he'd have to run the whole way home with the beast slung across his back.

He straddled its body to keep it still and covered its eyes with one hand as he slit its throat. It bucked once, then quivered for a bit before slumping, warm and lifeless, beneath him. He held it up by its hind legs to weigh it, struggling to hold it aloft. It must have been fifty pounds; it would be hell to carry back. The sun had disappeared completely behind the ridge and the air had begun to cool as dusk approached. He'd have to risk drawing the attention of wolves by trailing blood behind him as he ran, but they were cowardly creatures, and they knew the threat of his sling. The wild men of the canyons knew no fear, and a lone stranger would draw them like moths to a flame.

He hefted the beast onto his shoulders and scanned the horizon in the direction of the canyons to make sure he was not being watched. His heart nearly leapt from his chest when he saw the figure silhouetted against the snowy peaks in the distance.

They stood straight and tall, pale eyes watching him from the shadows of their hood. Their gray cloak matched the rock littering the mountainside. A long scabbard hung at their side, and a bow was slung over their shoulder, along with a pack and quiver. A pair of bats twirled in the sky behind them. Their eyes seemed to narrow for a moment, then with a whirl of their cloak, they disappeared. Later,

Dralen would surmise they were standing on a rock or hillock and had simply jumped down, or perhaps had stepped behind a boulder. But in that moment, it appeared that they simply vanished into thin air.

In any case, Dralen did not stick around to find out. He started running at top speed, heedless of the nildeer's blood dripping down his leg and inside his boot, unconcerned about the thought of wolves or bats or even Logans. It wasn't until he had crossed Fickle Creek that he began to slow his pace since the light was sticking around longer than expected. Or perhaps he'd run faster than he thought; the appearance of the mysterious cloaked stranger had certainly set fire to his steps. The nildeer had grown heavy, and the blood in his boot had cooled and was sticky and uncomfortable. But at this point, he was so close to home that there was nothing to do but keep trudging and deal with it when he got back. Along with cleaning the deer, fetching the water, helping with his grandfather, and gods knew how many other tasks that awaited him as always.

But he had gone hunting and come back with a nildeer. Even his mother couldn't say he hadn't earned his keep today.

"Thought the Logans had got you." Dralen's mother frowned through the open doorway, but the lines on her face eased when she saw the deer he'd hung under the eaves of the shed. "That's a nice one."

She stepped inside, and he heard her holler 'Dralen got a fat nildeer,' and his Urpa's grunted response. She emerged with a lantern and the chipped bowl they used to sort the organs into. She hung the lantern and helped him skin the creature, neither of them exchanging a word as they worked. When they'd finished and rinsed their hands, he nodded to her, and she squatted with one hand on the basin.

"Where'd you get it?"

"Over by Fishback Ridge." Dralen made a long cut down the animal's stomach, picturing the cloaked figure watching him as he stood from his kill.

"Hells, Dralen, I was kidding about the Logans, but isn't that cutting it a bit close?"

Dralen sighed, setting down the knife to widen the cut a little with his fingers.

"Wounded her and she ran off on me." He picked the knife back up and began the butchery, wincing with regret as he realized the blade wasn't quite as sharp as he wanted it to be. "Had to chase her almost to the canyons."

"Dralen Solomel!"

Dralen clenched his teeth, his mother's use of his middle name grating like the blade as he cut too deep and hit bone. He felt his father's name in her tone, the unspoken reproach when he did anything remotely risky, like living on a mountain. It's not like he could just avoid ravines entirely.

"You know I'm always careful, Ma." He wiped the knife and his hands on the already bloody rag. She harumphed.

"I ain't him," he muttered as he carefully slid the mass of organs and fat down into the basin.

"That you ain't," she said softly, sorting the edible parts into the bowl.

Dralen's ears burned. How the hells was he supposed to take that? He scraped out the remainder of the fat with Urpa's little curved knife, thinking how it was really his knife now that Urpa was stuck in that chair for the rest of his life.

"I'll get some water boiling to clean up." His mother's voice was quiet, without the edge it often had. Dralen glanced up from his task to see an almost wistful glint in her eye. By the time he'd composed his face to smile at her, she'd disappeared back into the house.

Urpa's fingers clutched Dralen's arm as he moved to stand from his chair to head for bed, overlong nails digging into his flesh through his sleeve.

"You've got a story to tell."

Dralen forced a little laugh. "I told you already. Just a nildeer I hit on the nose that ran off toward the canyons. I barely caught it before the bats came out. Had to run all the way back with it bleeding down my leg and into my boot."

Urpa's grip softened, but he didn't let go.

"You told me that part." He licked his lips, put his extinguished pipe to them, puffed a few times, and set it down. "You left something out."

Dralen's cheeks flushed. Urpa did a good job of seeming witless when it suited him, but he hadn't lost his uncanny talent for sussing out half-truths. Dralen could either maintain the lie and suffer days of silent judgment or tell about the cloaked figure, knowing it would send Urpa into one of his endless stories. As he pictured the figure's pale eyes staring at him from the darkness of their hood, he felt the pull of those tales that had so enchanted him as a child. Urpa coughed, a wet, ugly sound like a goat struggling to give birth. Perhaps he should indulge the old man after all. He cocked his ear toward the bedroom, where he heard his mother's gentle snoring.

"Promise to tell no one."

"Who would believe a delusional old man?"

Dralen nodded, picking up Urpa's pipe, tapping it out, and reloading it. He wiped off the stem on his sleeve, lit it with a stick from the fire, and took a few puffs before passing it to his grandfather, who beamed thanks. Urpa wasn't supposed to be smoking in his condition, but in his condition, what did it matter anyway?

"I saw someone today out by the canyons. A stranger in a gray cloak, with a sword and bow."

The crackle of the pipe rose over the hiss of the fire. Urpa coughed, then took another slow draw, letting the smoke out through his nose, with only a muffled cough this time. They sat in silence for a long moment until Urpa intoned:

"When the Earth's final breath blows forth from the hills,
  They of the West will return
  In search of treasures buried
  In memory's mine."

Chills raced over Dralen's body despite the stuffy warmth of the room. Urpa was a bottomless well of old songs and stories, and Dralen had heard most of them before, but he was sure he'd never heard this one.

"What's that from?"

Urpa took another draw from his pipe and coughed it out, gripping Dralen's arm so fiercely he worried his nails would draw blood. When the coughing had subsided, the old man turned rheumy eyes to Dralen, a weary smile on his wet lips.

"It's from an old poem my brother told me before the cave-in took him." He paused, put the pipe to his lips, then set it down. "I can't remember the rest. He was even more of a storyteller than me. You would have liked him."

Dralen's mother had only spoken ill of great uncle Verg, so Dralen was sure he'd have loved him. To hear his mother tell it, Verg loved to sing, dance, tell stories, play games with the children, and do anything but an honest day's work. Dralen knew from Urpa's stories that Verg had made his living finding topaz in the canyons, where most miners didn't dare to venture. He'd met his end mining there, buried in a cave-in, though his body had never been recovered for fear of the Logans.

"So, you think this poem is some kind of...prophecy or something?" Both Urpa and Verg were thought to have the sight; Dralen wasn't sure he believed in it, but he wasn't sure he didn't.

Urpa barked a laugh, which turned into a cough before morphing back into a laugh.

"Gods forbid. It's just a tangle of words meant to inspire us to find meaning where there is none. But if we look hard enough, we can find meaning in almost anything, hmm? And once we find meaning, who cares where it came from?" He winked at Dralen, then took a draw on his pipe, which was extinguished. "Verg said he heard it from a traveler, but you know? I always wondered if he wrote it himself." He smiled weakly, glancing toward the fire, then closed his eyes and set the pipe down on the table. His grip on Dralen's wrist relaxed, and in time Dralen slipped out of his grasp and made his way to the cot in the corner where he slept.

Urpa's words swirled around in his mind, along with images of the hooded figure, keeping sleep at bay until deep into the night. *They of the West,* Verg's poem had said. The figure certainly hadn't come from the east, since there was nothing but uninhabited mountains in that direction, and someone would have spotted Them if They'd come in from the east anyway. Dralen chuckled to himself as he capitalized the T in his mind. Something about the way Urpa said the word made it sound like a name rather than a group of people. And in truth, he wasn't really sure if They were a man or a woman. He's assumed man because of the sword, but the more he thought about it, the less sure he was. He chewed on that thought for a moment, then let it go as other words of the poem flowed through his mind.

The Earth's final breath

The dragon winds had blown through not a week before, bringing hot, dry weather that made spring feel like the dead of summer. Legends said they would herald the end of days, though since they came every year, it was hard to take that sign too seriously.

In search of treasures buried
In memory's mine

He and the other kids had always made up stories about treasures buried in the canyons; it was a forbidden place, so of course that's where treasure would be found in some creepy legend. The bit about memory's mine was confusing, but it was just an old poem after all. Like Urpa said, he was just trying to find meaning where there was none.

But the cloaked figure wasn't there by accident.

No one came to the Scrublands without a good reason, and there were precious few of those. If They were looking for someone, They'd have come to one of the villages instead of skulking in the hills, and news of such a visitor would have traveled fast. Their proximity to the canyons couldn't have been a coincidence, nor the fact that They were armed for battle. He wondered if They knew what They were getting into. However skilled They might be with Their sword and bow, They were one person. If a band of Logans fell upon Them, They wouldn't stand a chance.

2

"Jaela, mind the littles. We're going to Council."

Jaela bit her snarl into something like a smile. Council was just an excuse to dump the littles on the eldest child and go drinking, as there hadn't been anything to decide in more than a year.

"Of course, Mami."

"Give Teeki a honey drop if she cries for too long. She's—"

"Yes, I know, her teeth. Just go." She handed her mother the flask and pushed her gently toward the door. "Papi will be waiting."

Mami put a soft hand on Jaela's shoulder, a flash of almost-apology in her eyes, then she was gone.

"Can we play Bats and Logans?" Georgi jumped up and down, her hands forming into claws as her mouth stretched wide to show her pointy little teeth. "I'll be the Logan!"

"And we'll be the bats! Come on, Teeki!" Brin took the wide-eyed toddler by the chubby hand and dragged her through the open doorway. Jaela covered her eyes with her hand.

"Don't go past the Jenson's fence!" she called after them. "Georgi, it's your hide if you do!"

Georgi responded by stomping, wide-legged, with Logan claws outspread, and Brin and Teeki flapped their arms and disappeared between the Jenson's house and the chicken coop.

Jaela sighed at the mess around the dinner table. Teeki's spot was smeared with bits of crumbled egg yolk and the goatleaf she always spat out, no matter how many times Mami insisted on serving it to her. Brin at least was a fastidious eater, leaving her uneaten stems in a neat row like stacked logs. Georgi had devoured every scrap as usual, picking up stray crumbs with her fingers and pressing them to her lips.

Jaela poured herself a dram of whisky from the cask and downed it, gasping at the burn as she surveyed the drudgery ahead of her. If she was old enough to be in charge of cleaning the house and taking care of the littles while her parents went out drinking, surely she deserved a little liquid solace. In truth, it soured her stomach more than it buoyed her spirits, but it fueled her spite as she wiped, rinsed, wrung, and wiped again.

When she dumped the filthy bucket behind the house, she called out into the gathering dusk:

"Georgi, Brin, Teeki, get your rickety butts back in here this instant!"

"The bats aren't out yet!" Brin's shrill voice called out from behind the coop.

"But the Logans are!" Georgi lurched toward the coop, arms splayed wide, and Brin dragged Teeki squealing through the yard and into the house, with Georgi hot on their tail.

Jaela crossed her arms and blocked the doorway. Georgi flashed her teeth and claws once more before sulking back to normal shape and slinking through the door. Jaela steeled her jaw; she'd played Bats and Logans as much as any kid, but since her close encounter last year, it creeped her out more than she let on and she didn't allow it inside the house.

It took her more than an hour and five stories to get all of her siblings into bed. She snuck another dram from the cask and slipped around the back of the house with her pipe, hoping none of the nosy neighbors would notice. Most were at Council anyway, and Ms. Jenson usually turned in early, but the last thing she needed was another excuse for her mother to load extra chores on her. She'd be up before dawn to help get the cattle out to pasture, then back to make lunch for the littles while her parents pressed cheese. She couldn't wait until Georgi was a little older so she could take some of the load, but her parents would surely have Jaela taking over the cheesemaking by then so they could spend even more time at Council.

"Spare a puff?"

Jaela almost jumped as Dralen sidled out from behind the woodpile.

"I thought you didn't smoke."

She handed him her pipe, and he took a long draw. Let it out. Took another, then handed it back.

"I don't, as a rule."

Jaela grunted a laugh. Dralen's 'rule' was that he only smoked other people's pipes, but between his Urpa and Jaela and anyone else who happened to be around, he smoked plenty. But she stole her tarweed from her parents, so she couldn't exactly complain.

"Littles in bed?"

Jaela nodded, letting the smoke curl out of the corner of her mouth.

"Finally."

"Parents still at Council?"

"Until the whisky runs out. I sent Mami with a full flask, and Papi always packs one too."

"Then you'll have time to hear me out."

Jaela's pipe hung inches from her lips. She eyed Dralen, who stared off into the distance. This wasn't his usual I've-got-a-story tone, or his My-mother-doesn't-value-my-contributions-to-our-household tone, or even his My-grandfather-is-really-sick-and-I'm-worried tone. This was a tone she hadn't heard since they were kids running wild in the hills, and it sparked a fire deep in Jaela's chest. She took a long draw off her pipe and turned to face him.

"Tell me."

3

Once he'd finished his story and laid out his plan, Dralen drew on the pipe, which was mostly ash by now, and handed it back to Jaela.

"Just like that?" The worry in her tone was laced with curiosity and more than a little eagerness.

"I've gone out to the east foraging for medicinal herbs for Urpa before. No Logans that way anyhow, so she shouldn't worry. And I should be able to bring back some hushreeds from the little marsh below the canyons. She won't know the difference, and she'll be glad to have me out of her hair for a bit anyway."

"And how is it exactly you plan to not get gobbled up by Logans in the canyons?"

Dralen sucked his teeth, went to spit, and swallowed it instead. That part was still a little hazy.

"I can hit a man with a sling bullet at fifty yards, and I can reload and shoot every five seconds. Not to mention I can outrun anyone I've ever met."

"So, you're just gonna leave me behind if things get tough?"

Jaela's big bright eyes radiated into his.

"I'm not asking you to come with me, Jae."

"Well, you sure as shit ain't going alone. And besides, I can keep 'em at bay with my bullwhip, and we both know I'm twice the foot fighter you are."

Dralen started to laugh, but she wasn't wrong. Jaela's bulging thighs and quick strikes had laid low every boy in the village, and most of the men who'd dared to step into the ring with her. Not that he thought the Logans would respect the rules of the sport, but she could more than hold her own in a fight.

"You're pretty fast too, for being as short as you are."

He stifled a cry as her foot swept his legs from beneath him and her palm tapped his chest, sending him thudding to the dirt.

"Dragons' guts, Jaela! Okay, you can go! But what'll you tell your Mami?"

"I'll tell her she can raise her own damned kids for a couple days, that's what."

"I'm telling!" Georgi's sing-song whine sounded from the corner of the house. The smirk drained from her face, along with all of her color, as Jaela snatched her up and slammed her against the woodpile, scattering logs and pinning her flailing limbs as she bared her teeth in her little sister's panic-stricken face.

"If you so much as breathe a word of whatever it is you think you heard, I'll pull your guts out your backside and tie them round your neck," Jaela hissed in a voice that set Dralen's teeth on edge. Jaela had a violent streak that made him want to cry right along with Georgi, who nodded, a fat tear sliding down her cheek. Jaela lowered her gently to the ground, wiping her cheek and brushing a bit of bark from her nightgown.

"You're going to have to be the big sister around here sometimes. Best you be ready."

Georgi nodded again, glancing between Dralen and her feet with big wet eyes.

Jaela squeezed her shoulders and kissed her forehead.

"Now why don't you go inside and make sure the littles are sound asleep."

Dralen let out a long breath when Georgi had gone. Jaela held up a finger to stop him from saying what he was smart enough not to say.

"She likes to pretend she's still just a kid, but she can handle the other two by herself for a day or two. That's all we're talking about, right?"

"Just a day or two. Just long enough to figure out what the heck They're doing in those canyons."

Jaela repacked her pipe and lit it, puffing aggressively for a while before handing it to Dralen. It was too hot, but he took a small puff anyway, watching Jaela slowly cool down. It was funny; she acted more like a man than he did. More like a man than he ever wanted to be. Not that he cared; he hadn't met many men except his Urpa that were worth imitating.

"I can bring a hunk of cheese and maybe some dried apples," Jaela said, staring at the stars that had just started popping now that the sky was fully dark.

"I can nab some day-old bread and a bit of jerky, and I'm sure to catch us something along the way."

"I'll slip out past the Beetle Horn once the cows are at pasture. I'll leave a note saying I'm off east helping you get medicine for your Urpa and I'll be back in a couple of days. If they want to raise a fuss, they'll have to do it when we get back."

Dralen sucked his teeth, wishing he could spit the acrid taste of the tarweed out of his mouth, but he always hated when his Urpa did it, so he vowed never to do it when anyone was around. Jaela's mother would surely come bothering his, and it would be hard to explain why he needed Jaela's help, but that was a problem for after.

There was no time to waste; the cloaked figure was surely in the canyons by now and had no doubt run across the Logans already. With Their sword and bow, maybe They were still alive, but that didn't answer his most pressing questions. Why had They come? What treasures were buried in memory's mine?

4

Jaela made her excuses while the other hands had stopped for lunch. She made the rendezvous point at Beetle's Horn and found Dralen waiting for her, whittling a piece of soft wood into one of the little knights he was always carving.

"I thought maybe you'd think better of it and stay with the cows."

"And let you have all the fun? Fuck that. Let's do this."

"I found lunch."

He tossed her a slightly over-ripe bush pear, which she devoured as they walked. It was almost sickly sweet, but she was hungry, and she licked every bit of the sap from her fingers before tossing the skin. Dralen stopped, picked up the skin, and tossed it farther from the trail down into a nearby ravine.

"In case they come looking for us. Don't want to make it easy on them."

"Hell, Dralen, ain't no one gonna come after us."

"Not if we come back when we said, probably not."

"And if they do, they'll go look east, right?"

"That's where we said we were going, yeah."

"So, if we're gone more than a few days and they go looking east, they ain't gonna find us. And if they figure it out and come looking this way, by then, maybe we'll want them to find us. Maybe we *should* leave a trail."

Dralen stopped, hands balled at his waist.

"You never leave a trail, Jae. *Never.* That's the only rule."

"The only rule of what, Drale?" Jaela's voice rose a bit, and she lowered it as she saw the hard glint of Dralen's eyes. She'd wanted to challenge him a moment ago, just on principle, but now she wasn't so sure.

"Let's just keep going, okay? We're a little exposed until we get past this ridge, so keep low while we have the cover of the bramble."

He lowered to a crouch and picked up the pace so she didn't have time to respond, not that she could think of anything to say. Dralen was the gentlest soul she knew, but once in a while, he just got ornery out of nowhere and ran off for a while to mull over whatever was gnawing at him. Best to let him be, she supposed.

Dralen's pace eased once they crested the ridge and descended into a sun-beaten valley dotted with wire bush and fireflowers, blazing red and yellow against the dusty brown of the hills. He led them down to the narrow line of birches along a creek, swollen by the glacier melt from the dragon winds. Jaela's throat was parched, and she looked to Dralen hopefully as he crouched, cupping the water in his hands and sniffing it.

"It's probably safe to drink with the extra melt if you're thirsty, but I wouldn't fill my waterskin. There's a spring we'll reach near dusk, a few hours from the lower canyons, where we can fill our skins and hole up for the night."

Dralen didn't drink, but Jaela took off her boots, cooled her feet, and drank her fill with cupped hands as he stood watch, ever eyeing the horizon. He never glanced at her until she was re-shod and refreshed and had clambered out of the creek. She wondered if he ever thought of her the way she thought of some of the girls in the village, or if he thought of boys that way, or if he thought of anyone that way. It wasn't really her business; it wasn't a big deal; she was a little curious, was all.

"If you're ready, we should get moving. I'd like to set up camp before dark."

She followed behind him, not asking what 'set up camp' meant. Dralen slept out of doors sometimes, and while it didn't sound very comfortable, the thrill of adventure made her feet light and quelled the growing hunger in her belly. She'd lived in the dim shadow of her family's little house in Graueck for more than fifteen years, and this was the first time she could remember not knowing where she would wake up the next morning. It was exhilarating.

As he rounded the edge of a bramble, Dralen crouched, motioning for her to stop, and unwound his sling. She tensed, trying to see through the bramble, but all she saw was brown dust and rock dotted with more bramble and a few clumps of ironflowers. Dralen adjusted his stance, whirling his sling silently for a moment, then released it. A brief scrabble of rock sounded down the hill, and she spotted a puff of dust through the branches of the bramble. Dralen's face lit up, and he took off running, with Jaela hot on his heels. He skidded to a halt next to the limp, dusty corpse of a rock hare with a bloody hole where one of its eyes should have been. A half-chewed ironflower dangled from its mouth, pale blue and covered in bloody saliva. Jaela's stomach roiled for a moment, and she steeled herself against the sudden urge to vomit.

"Damn, Drale. I knew you were a good shot, but...damn."

"We'll need to cook it before dark, but I doubt anyone from the village will be out this far, and I don't think the Logans would be out to see it during daylight hours. Best to save what little food we brought."

He dusted the pathetic creature, which looked like a bloody rag doll, stuffed it in a pouch, and gestured toward the ravine ahead.

"Just an hour to go before we reach the spring, and a good couple hours after that before dusk. We should just have time."

Jaela sucked the last of the grease from her fingers, savoring the salt and herb mix Dralen had seasoned the hare with. Pepper, rosemary, fireflower root, and something else she couldn't quite place. She studied her fingers as if they could tell her what the mystery ingredient was.

"Wild fennel?" she asked.

Dralen cracked a smile, nodding.

"It grows in the lower valleys. Harvested some on a trip a couple years back with my cousins. The seeds keep remarkably well." He kicked dirt over the remaining coals, which were no longer smoking, and eyed the dimming sky. "Best get some brush for bedding before dusk hits." The tone in his voice dropped, and Jaela's neck prickled as visions of her run-in with the Logans a year before rushed through her head.

She'd been out chasing a stray calf that had been spooked by hilldogs. It had run off over a ridge and scampered down a long ravine that led toward the upper canyons. It was her fault; she'd been jawing with two of the other hands and hadn't noticed the calf straying, hadn't seen the line of hilldogs until they were almost upon the poor creature. If the calf had just stayed put or run back toward them, it would have been in no danger. Half a dozen hilldogs couldn't take down a healthy calf unless they frightened it into falling down a ravine and breaking a leg. Which was the idea, she supposed, and it had nearly worked.

She'd chased the beast until her lungs burned and her legs ached. It had finally stopped at the bottom of the ravine, heaving for breath and frothing at the mouth. The hilldogs had given up the chase once they'd seen her coming, and she'd managed to calm the calf down and regain her breath when she noticed how low the light was. She saw the first bat fly out from an overhang near the base of the ravine, followed by dozens more. She hadn't been down this way before, but she knew she was dangerously close to the canyons cut by the glacier streams.

Her blood chilled when she heard it, at once a human sound and something entirely *other*.

It had a mournful, almost songlike quality, rising from a low moan to a high, plaintive note, soon joined by another, and another, echoing off the walls of the ravine in irregular patterns. The calf's ears twitched and its hooves scrabbled on the scree as it spun around, nearly knocking Jaela to the ground. She saw the figures emerge in the dim light of dusk, one by one, more lurching than running, as if they were still learning how to use their bodies, stretching them to feel their extremities for the first time. They wore clothes of some kind—rags, it seemed to her in the half-second she saw them before she turned and ran—but it was their faces that remained fixed in her memory: eyes wide with surprise, pain, delight—it was impossible to tell—mouths full of yellowed teeth stretched wide in their unearthly howls.

"You all right, Jae?" Dralen's voice was soft with concern as he dropped a huge armful of brush at her feet.

"Yeah." She shook her head to clear it. "Yeah." She studied the sky to the west, which the sun had painted in swaths of deep crimson and purple. "Bats come out yet?"

"Should be any time now."

She felt for her pipe, wishing for a smoke, realizing this was not the time.

"Don't worry, Jae. The Logans won't come down this way. They follow the upper canyons, from what I heard. I picked this spot because it's between the hills. We should be safe here." He sounded a little bit like he was trying to convince himself.

"I'm not worried, Drale. I'm just wondering, is all."

"You've got good instincts. You'd make a good hunter."

"And there they come." Jaela's heart sank as she saw the first bat squiggling through the sky, followed by another. Swallows joined them in their feast, picking the evening insects from the air. Jaela wished they'd feed closer to the ground, as the drainflies had started harassing her, forcing her to cover her exposed skin. It was still warm in the wake of the dragon winds, but warm was better than hot, and better than bitten to death.

They sat in silence, listening for the Logans' wailing, but they heard only the howls of distant wolves and the gurgling of the little spring. After a while, Dralen spread out his blanket on his pile of brush, and Jaela did the same. It took some rolling around to crush the prickly bits down, and it wasn't much padding against the hard ground. But when she thought of the sound of her parents snoring or fucking and her siblings fighting and the smell of cheese and farting and the weight of the responsibilities she'd have woken up to back home, she settled in quite comfortably and sleep soon carried her off.

5

Dralen was awake before dawn, listening to the familiar sounds of the mountain: the scrub wren's brash trill; the whisper of breeze in the brush; the stream's steady gurgle. Jaela's faint snore, like a disgruntled cat's purr, was the only unfamiliar noise, but it was a comforting disturbance. He liked being alone, but he found being alone with Jaela pleasant, especially considering the circumstances. He slipped from his blanket to relieve himself well clear of the spring, noting a gray tone to the sunrise that might herald rain before the day was over. That was the last thing they needed in the canyons, which could fill up in a heartbeat in a heavy downpour.

He let Jaela sleep until dawn, then woke her by not so quietly dismantling his bedding and clearing the traces of their fire. If anyone came looking, they'd see the evidence up close, but they wouldn't notice from a distance. He still wasn't sure if they'd want to be found. Maybe Jaela was right; if they were gone more than a few days, folks would be right to come looking for them, and at that point, they might be glad to be missed.

"Looks like rain later." Jaela finished the last bite of cheese and took the stale crust Dralen offered her, twisting it sideways in her teeth as she studied the gray-limned horizon.

"It might pass to the north, but we'll keep an eye on it."

"How long did you say til we reach the lower canyons?"

"Two, three hours."

Jaela nodded, stuffing the last bit of bread in her mouth, looking at her hands as if they might contain more food. She was normally a big eater; he'd been worried about supplies, but she hadn't complained about being hungry yet. And they still had her apples and his jerky. He was sure he could catch or forage something if it came to it.

"And once we get there..." She stared off toward the west, letting the words hang in the air as her messy ponytail stirred in the breeze. Dralen had been half hoping she wouldn't ask, since he didn't have much of an answer prepared.

"I figure I can track Them easy enough. We'll cross over where I last saw Them in a bit, and once we get into the canyons, the dust doesn't get disturbed too much. Tracks tend to stay put."

"You've been there?" Jaela's voice rose with curiosity.

Dralen nodded, went to spit, didn't.

"Once, with my uncle. He took me to a side canyon on a snake hunt, for snake-bite medicine. Crazy son of a bear caught a rock viper with nothing more than a hooked stick and a leather bag. Anyway, you could see their tracks in the sand inside the canyons since the rain doesn't fall in there. So, I figure we can at least see where They entered, see what to do from there."

Jaela nodded, took a drink from her waterskin, then squinted at him.

"You keep saying 'They' all funny, like it's their name or something."

Dralen bit back his spit again. He'd taken to thinking of Them that way, in part because he wasn't sure if They were a he or a she. He found it pleasing to think of Them as neither, or as both at the same time somehow. He'd heard that there were people in Fenylbyr who lived as the opposite gender of what they were raised as, and even some who lived as something in between, whatever that meant. The idea had always intrigued him. And something about the way Urpa had said it stuck in his mind. He hadn't told Jaela about this part, but it seemed like the time had come.

"It's something Urpa said. When I told him about the hooded figure. He got that weird tone of his and started reciting lines from this old poem my great uncle Verg apparently told him. Something about *When the Earth breathes its last breath, They of the West will come in search of treasure buried in memory's mine.*"

"Dragon's guts and bloody diarrhea, Dralen!" Jaela shoved him hard in the chest, and he staggered back a few steps. She was as strong as a bull, strong enough that it scared him sometimes. "Why the fuck didn't you tell me?"

"Calm your shit, Jaela, or we're going back." Dralen rubbed his chest, taking a cautious step toward her. Whatever had gotten into her, he wasn't going to stand there and take it. She might be strong, and a tough foot fighter, but he was taller and older, and he wasn't about to be bullied by anyone, least of all his best friend. "Urpa says all kinds of crazy shit. I didn't want to get you all excited about some mythical 'treasure' or anything. We're not kids anymore. You turn sixteen in what, three months?"

Jaela nodded, sucking her teeth. She relaxed her posture and huffed out a sigh.

"I'm sorry I pushed you, Drale. I shouldn't have done that. I just—" She balled her hands into fists. "You can't keep shit like that from me! Your Urpa knows things, and probably your great uncle Verg did, too. Hell, maybe you do. They say it runs in the family."

"I don't know anything." Dralen spun away, kicking the dirt. No one in the family had ever talked to him directly about having the sight, but he'd overheard his mother talking to Urpa about it a couple of times. "I even tried, plenty. Whatever it is you think they got—I don't."

He flinched at Jaela's hand on his shoulder, then leaned into it.

"Maybe you do. Maybe yours works different'n theirs. Maybe that's why you knew we had to come out here."

Dralen sniffled, wiping his eyes in a gesture meant to hide what he was doing. Not that Jaela would have minded. It was just a stupid habit, playing tough. Half the reason he loved being out by himself was so he didn't have to. He half-turned, putting a hand on her thick bicep.

"Maybe that's why I didn't tell you until now." He still didn't believe it, not really. But when he thought back to the moment he'd seen Them, some part of his brain lit up deep down in a way that was eerily familiar, if too vague to get ahold of.

"Well, if you get any more of your little instincts or whatever, I want you to tell me, hear? You may not believe in it, but I do." Her meaty hand clamped down on the nerve in his shoulder, and he slunk out of her grip.

"Anyway, let's have a drink and fill our skins, then get a little closer and see what we can see. We should be within sight of the canyons in an hour."

They lay flat atop the ridge, studying the shadowy gray canyons that snaked down from the glaciers on the peaks above. Here and there water glittered through the deep cuts in the rock, but in most places Forked Creek was invisible until it let out onto the granite fields of the lower hills, where it forked, rejoined, and forked again, earning its name a dozen times over.

There was no movement and nothing obvious to see near the lower entrance, though at this distance it would be easy to miss something. He'd been saving up for a field scope like the one his uncle had, but he rarely got any coin, except when he brought home a slickback. Their fur would fetch a couple hundred rabble apiece, and his mother let him split it with her since they were a rare and prized catch that brought a month's worth of income in a single day.

"I can't see a damned thing down there." Jaela sat up, taking a swig of her waterskin. Dralen resisted the urge to tell her to wait; he wasn't sure whether the water in the canyons was safe to drink, and it was a long hike down and back up.

"I don't see anything either. We'll have to get closer in. I was thinking we head around the side of that smaller canyon there, to the east, and follow the line of trees for cover. That might let us get close enough to see something we can't make out from here."

"It's your show, Dralen." She corked her skin and looked at him expectantly.

He led her along the ridge, down a game trail that wound through some boulders for a little cover, then through a scrubby open area to the thin forest near the edge of a side canyon, shallower than the main one. He motioned for Jaela to wait as he crept toward the edge and looked down. A steady stream of water flowed between slabs of broken rock no more than twenty feet down, leading toward the main canyon. He saw no signs of movement other than the water and no signs of human or animal activity. There were a few places below where a person could pick their way through if they were careful, but it would be treacherous going.

"Not much to see down there. Maybe twenty feet deep on average. I guess we move as quietly as we can through these trees and get on top there near the main entrance and take a peek down."

"I brought some rope, about forty feet. How deep do you think the main canyons are?"

"Fifty feet deep at least, probably more in spots, from what I've heard. There are some caves underneath as well, that the river uncovered over the centuries as it carved its way through the soft stone."

"Neat." Jaela's tone was half enthusiastic, half fearful, and Dralen shared the sentiment.

"Let me go a little bit ahead, just in case."

"I'll keep you in bullwhip distance."

Dralen wasn't quite sure what that meant, or whether it was meant to be reassuring, but he flashed a smile, softened his feet, and made his way through the trees. He stopped as he approached where the smaller canyon met the main one. The treeline petered out within about twenty feet of the main canyon. He scanned the area all around until he was sure it was empty of everything except a few ground sparrows, then lowered down on all fours and crawled to the edge.

The rush of the creek echoed up off smooth, rounded walls, but the channel had shifted over the eons, so he couldn't actually see the water from here. He scouted the best route down if he were to climb it, not that he planned to; the rock looked solid and stable, though without too many footholds. It would be tough going without rope, and a fall would be costly. He crawled along the edge, cursing under his breath as his hand dislodged a pebble that clattered its way from wall to wall into the rush of water below. He lay flat and still for a long time, hoping the sound of the water had covered the pebble if there was even anyone there to hear it. After he heard no further noise, he turned back toward Jaela, who was distractedly picking berries off a scrub holly at the treeline. It took a moment to catch her attention, but she quickly got down on all fours and joined him, raising a bit more dust than he would have liked.

"We could get down there in a pinch," she said a little too loudly, glancing down into the canyon. "Though there aren't too many places up here to attach a rope."

"We're up here to look, not to climb. We'll worry about that later." He kept his voice low, hoping she'd take the hint. She nodded, touching a finger to her lips. He nodded toward the lower canyon mouth, about a mile away, where they'd be able to look down from fifty feet above the entrance and surrounding landscape and see what kind of tracks were around.

They made their way in a crouch, since it was too far to crawl, stopping periodically to glance down into the twisting crevices that yawned to their right. At one point, he thought he heard voices. He stopped and listened as hard as he could, but he couldn't make out anything above the noise of the water. He was just imagining it.

As they neared the edge where the canyons tumbled onto the granite fields below, they crouched behind an outcropping so Dralen could take stock of the situation and catch a breath. His chest felt tight, and his vision had begun to cloud around the edges. He just needed to rest and relax his mind a bit, was all.

"This is kind of exciting," Jaela whispered, peering around the edge of the boulder. "Just like when we were kids playing Treasure Castle, right?"

Dralen had to stifle the laugh that burst through his chest, loosening his anxiety a little and pushing the clouds back. Jaela had always been the one to rush into the barn, even when she knew the Braden boys were waiting in the loft to pounce down on her as soon as she entered. And she'd wrestle the two of them while the others got the old mail shirt they used as treasure, often besting two boys twice her age and size through sheer tenacity.

"We're going to take it slow now, Jae. We're not kids anymore."

"I know, Drale, you don't have to keep saying it." She puffed her annoyance, but curiosity quickly wiped it from her face. "What are you expecting to see anyway?"

"Well, I don't know if *They* would have come through the main entrance or one of the side canyons, but I'm guessing They're the type to get right to the matter. I'm expecting to see Their tracks. Long, steady strides. Boot tracks, big, but not too big, come to think of it." Dralen scratched his sideburns. They had certainly presented an imposing figure with their cloak and weaponry, but They hadn't actually been that tall, had They? It was hard to tell because of the distance and without any good landmarks, but come to think of it, he wasn't quite sure They were tall at all. Certainly not short, but maybe not any taller than he.

"What about Logan tracks? They'd be barefoot, I guess."

"I can only imagine."

"Irregular strides, I'd think. Like they don't control their bodies so good. Half walking, half running, confused and excited at the same time..." Jaela trailed off, her words leaving a chill between them. She'd mentioned her run-in to him, sworn him to secrecy, but hadn't said much about it other than that it was a close call.

"Are you sure you're up for this, Jae?" he asked cautiously, hoping she wouldn't flare up and shove him again.

She nodded somberly.

"I figure the only way to get rid of your fear is to face it."

"S'what they say."

"And besides, we ain't going in there at night, right?"

"Not in a million years."

6

Jaela lay flat next to Dralen, who studied the crisscrossing tracks around the entrance for a long time without saying anything. She couldn't make much of them, but it seemed like an awful lot of tracks to her, much more than she would have expected, and more than just Logans and a hooded stranger, for sure.

"There's folks living in those canyons, Jaela."

"Logans?"

Dralen sucked his teeth, turning to face her.

"Maybe? But unless some of them wear shoes, I'd say no. Or not *just* Logans."

"What about...you know. *Them.*"

He shook his head. "I need to go down there to see the tracks up close." He winced. "It's awfully exposed."

"We could creep around the side or something." It didn't seem helpful, but she felt like she should say something.

"If we climb down back a ways, we could stay out of sight until we're right up on it. I still don't like it with the sunlight and all."

"You'd like it a lot worse at night, Drale. Either we go in by day or we go home. Unless you want to climb in through the top?"

He nodded. "You're right." Nodded again. "There doesn't seem to be anyone around right now anyway, so we can move more quickly. Like you said, we need to get down there well before dusk." He glanced at the sky; it was past noon, though not by much. An uncertain mass of gray was building on the horizon, though it was tough to tell how soon or how hard it would hit. Jaela's stomach growled audibly, which was embarrassing, but she couldn't deny her hunger much longer. Dralen offered her a stick of jerky without a word, though he didn't take one himself.

"Come on, Jae. I saw a way down not too far back."

They made their way down a boulder-slide and along the edge of a cliff that sank into nothing as they neared the lower canyon mouth. Dralen gestured her behind a rock with a view of the dark interior of the canyon, which was like a long tunnel with a creek rushing through it and a twisting ribbon of sky occasionally visible above. She was happy to stay put as he stalked forward, nose to the ground. He studied the tracks for a while, then stared into the canyon, glancing back at her every now and then. The air wafting out of the canyon was cool, but not as cool as she'd expected, and a little fishy as well. She could make out a beaten path across the creek, with footprints visible even to her untrained eyes.

As Dralen approached, he stopped, his eyes fixed on the shadows of the canyon, and slowly drew his sling from his belt. Jaela tensed, studying the darkness, but saw nothing. Dralen remained motionless for some time, then finally secured the sling back onto his belt and walked on soft feet toward Jaela.

"Was there someone?" Jaela whispered, her eyes darting toward the canyon but not turning her head in case anyone was watching.

Dralen's head twitched in what might have been a no.

"Trick of the light maybe. The creek casts weird shadows. But there are definitely people living in these canyons, or at least traveling through them on the regular. As recently as this morning."

The breeze wafting out of the canyon felt suddenly cool.

"What about..."

"There are a few barefoot tracks mixed among the boot tracks, a good few days old, so they're a little harder to make out, but they're there." He paused, looking down at his hand. "These are hide boots, what the hill tribes wear, not boots made in a city. I only saw one set of tracks like those."

"They?"

Dralen's mouth tightened as he nodded almost imperceptibly.

"They've been here." He glanced into the canyon. "Might still be in there for all I know."

He stared into the shadows for a long time, then turned hard eyes back to Jaela.

Whatever he was about to say, she was in. She would follow that look of purpose anywhere.

"What are we gonna do?"

"We're going in."

They picked their way along the gray rocks and shallows opposite the path, getting their boots wet, which was nice for a while, as Jaela's feet tended to get hot. After an hour or so of slow, waterlogged slogging, they started to chafe, and she was half tempted to take them off and feel her way through without them, sharp rocks be damned.

The canyon was over fifty feet wide in places but it narrowed to less than half that in others, with water rushing fast and hard between granite boulders. She noticed that the path on the other side of the creek had been worked in spots, with stairs made of stacked stones and wooden handholds along steep drops. Parts of the canyon were cavelike and dark, with only reflected light allowing them to see their way. When it opened up, they hurried through stripes of troubled sunlight from the yawning cracks in the earth above. Jaela could tell by the cast of the sky that the front was approaching, and she knew it was foremost on Dralen's mind as well. They slowed as they approached the spot where a side canyon entered the main one. The roof opened wide, and the entire junction was as brightly lit as the hills above, which was to say covered in a pall of gray light heralding an approaching storm. Jaela's stomach rumbled so loudly it echoed off the wall next to her.

Dralen side-eyed her, crouching next to the wall and offering her a stick of jerky.

"I don't like the look of that sky," he whispered, tearing off a piece of jerky with his teeth. "We don't want to be down here if it rains too hard."

Jaela nodded, closing her eyes as the salty flavor of the jerky filled her with a moment of pure joy.

"I'm guessing we don't want to go climbing up in plain sight either, but we don't want to go back and waste this whole trip, right?"

Dralen cracked a quarter-smile.

"That's about the short and long." He tore off another piece of jerky with his teeth, chewing thoughtfully. "I say once we finish our snack, I cross over and see if I can still see Their bootprints. If it looks like They went further in, we risk traveling along the path so we make better time. We should be able to make it to the next side canyon before the rain hits, and we can make our decision then. But it's a little risky. The safer bet would be to climb up now, make camp, and come back in tomorrow."

Jaela's heart raced as she gazed across the creek at the little path. They hadn't seen or heard anyone since they'd entered the canyon, but if they were going to run across someone, they'd be coming down the path.

Including the Logans.

They lived in the canyons. She'd seen them there with her own eyes. The canyon she'd seen them in was a few miles up, but they were all connected. Some of the hardness had gone out of Dralen's eyes, and Jaela glanced at the rocks of the side canyon. It wouldn't be that hard of a climb. There were plenty of ways up.

But then what? Go back home, answer a thousand questions about where she went and why, and for what? So she could come back from Dralen's little quest having found out exactly nothing, then live the rest of her life in her stupid fucking mountain village and marry some stupid boy and have stupid snotty children who would smear their food all over the table as she went off to Council to drink away her sorrows because she was a broken-down cheesemaker with too many kids?

"Fuck that. We came down here to find out what *They* are doing in the canyons, and we haven't found out shit. Get your bony ass over there and find us some tracks, Dralen."

Dralen's smile was suspicious but wider this time. He stuffed the end of his jerky into his mouth and pointed at her to stay. He studied the rocks in the creek for a moment, then leap-frogged across in two quick hops. She stared into the rushing water, hoping to gods she would prove half as nimble as he. A slip into the water could result in a broken ankle or worse, and getting out of the canyons before dark with an injury like that would be no easy feat.

Dralen summoned her with a *psst* before she had time to overthink it, and she followed his pattern, surprising herself by landing on the other side of the creek without mishap. Dralen's eyebrows raised, and Jaela stuck out her tongue.

"Stay about twenty feet back," he whispered.

Jaela nodded, though she wasn't sure how much she liked it. If something went down, she'd want to be close enough to help. Twenty feet was out of bullwhip range. She'd have to be ready to rush forward at any moment while staying quiet enough not to draw his impatient glare.

She kept as close as she dared, following Dralen along the well-beaten path, which wound up a set of boulders with flat rocks for stepping, too conveniently placed to be natural. The darkening sky twisted into view again as the curving mass of gray rock of the opposite wall fell away, revealing a wide cavern open to the sky. The creek had been diverted around a rectangular island with a variety of plants growing in neat rows, with wooden cages supporting some of them. Dralen stopped, motioning her to stay, and seemed to study the surroundings for a long time before motioning her forward. He moved quickly through the lit area, and Jaela struggled to keep up the pace without making a racket. She glanced at the garden as she passed; it looked to be mostly medicinal herbs and flowers rather than vegetables. She didn't imagine the amount of sunlight down here would be enough for proper crops, and there wasn't much land to begin with.

The canyon took on a tunnel-like aspect as they continued, narrowing to no more than twenty feet, with the dim ribbon of sky appearing and disappearing in the gloom. The creek rushed hard through this section, and the path was wet in spots. There were even handrails on one of the stairways overlooking a particularly steep waterfall. The air rising from the water was warmer here, much more so than she would have expected from a river like this.

There must have been a hot spring feeding in somewhere.

Dralen ducked suddenly as he reached the top of the stairs, then slipped under the railing and clung to the rocks below. His eyes bulged, urging Jaela to do the same. Her heart beat hard and out of sync as she slunk under the railing and lowered herself over the slick, rough rock, holding onto the edge with trembling fingers as she sought footholds with her boots. Low voices sounded as her feet scrambled to find purchase. She let out a breath and stretched her body a little bit more, and her toe hit solid rock. She eased herself down, finding another handhold, and a second, and soon she was safely, if not comfortably, a few feet below the edge of the stairs. She hoped whoever was approaching was too engaged in their conversation to look down.

They spoke in low voices in a language she couldn't understand. She didn't dare to glance up, didn't follow them with her eyes as they passed. She did nothing more than listen to their approaching and then receding footsteps and voices and pray to all the gods she'd never believed in that they wouldn't notice her clinging to the wet rocks beneath their feet.

When they were out of earshot, she dared a glance at Dralen, who had already climbed back onto the stairs and was crouching at the top, scanning in both directions. He gestured her up, which turned out to be much more difficult than getting down, but damned if she was going to ask for or accept Dralen's help.

There was a fishy smell in the air as she got to her feet and met Dralen at the top of the stairs.

"Did you see that?" he whispered.

Jaela shook her head, looking down in embarrassment. She hated not being as brave as Dralen.

"I got a look once they were down the stairs. They were carrying sacks of what must have been fish. And they wore valley-style robes."

Jaela nodded. In villages farther down the mountains, people tended to wear robes, but in Graueck and the other hill villages, pants and tunics were more common, except among the elderly.

"Where the hell are they getting sacks of fish?" she asked, the question bubbling up suddenly.

Dralen chewed on his cheek, shrugging. "Let's keep going and maybe we'll find out."

They wound their way through the canyon, which widened again, showing a darkening sky that had begun to spit rain. Dralen let his fingers drag in the water, and Jaela did the same. It was even warmer here than before, much more so than a typical mountain stream, but still cooler than the air.

"We should reach the next side canyon in half an hour or so, which ought to be plenty of time." Dralen eyed the canyon walls, which might be climbable, but it would be a stretch with the rock all wet. Jaela shot him what she hoped was a meaningful look: *We need to get out of here before the Logans come out.* He blinked understanding, and they continued into the next narrow stretch. She half hoped they'd run into another group of the canyon folk; it would be better than the alternative.

Jaela's mind spun with visions of Logans lurching down the path in front of them, or behind, their mournful cries echoing off the canyon walls. Dralen might be able to outrun them, but would she? Or would she trip and fall on the unfamiliar terrain and lay bleeding on the ground as they swarmed over her, wide eyes and filthy nails and yellow teeth closing in for their mad feast?

She closed the distance with Dralen, who scowled over his shoulder, but she didn't care. It was getting darker and darker, even in the sections of the canyon with a direct view of the sky, where the rain pattered in on them, chilling Jaela's skin and heart. Dralen stopped at the crest of another set of boulder-stairs in a dark section of wide canyon, crouching and gesturing Jaela forward.

She crept up to the top and crouched next to Dralen behind the cover of a large jagged rock. The stream cascaded down from a line of rocks that looked structurally supported, like a dam. The canyon continued to their right, but a lake opened to the left in a dark cavern the river must have uncovered as it churned through this rock millennia ago. Numerous figures stood in the water and along the shore, working with ropes, wicker cages, and long nets. They looked like valley folk to her, though it was hard to tell at this distance; they had lighter hair kept in short ponytails and most wore no beards. Fins surfaced in the water here and there, and she recognized them as sailbacks, a meaty fish mostly found in lakes lower down in the valleys, cured and smoked and kept against the long winters.

Dralen ducked down against the boulder out of sight of the fisherfolk.

"They don't seem like Logans to me, Drale."

He shook his head with a small smile.

"I think we can slip past them, though. They seem occupied."

Jaela wasn't so sure, though she'd been too busy watching the lake, the fish, and the fisherfolk to pay attention to the canyon beyond.

"If you say so."

"It's either that or go back and climb up that last open space. Your call." Dralen's eyes shone dark, and it wasn't just the light. It *was* her call, but it was his quest, and she was with him all the way. She gave a tight nod, and Dralen's eyes crinkled around the edges. He peeked over the top again, then immediately climbed over and started moving with the grace of a mountain cat. Jaela followed, wincing as her boot scraped against the edge, but the sound of the waterfall surely drowned it out. She didn't dare watch anything except for Dralen's figure silhouetted against the gray ahead and the hazy outline of the path at her feet as she followed him past the lake and into the narrow confines of the canyon beyond.

The air grew quickly cooler; the hot spring must have fed into the lake, and the water from the creek here had the icy glacier breeze wafting off it. The ceiling opened briefly for long enough to let in a steady torrent of rain before twisting closed again. Water ran down the curving walls in sheets, and though the creek had not yet begun to visibly swell, it was only a matter of time. The path grew slick in spots where stones had been laid out to level it, and Jaela almost slipped into the rushing water more than once. After a long half-hour, the sound of roaring water was accompanied by a slight increase in the light, and they entered another open area, though the ominous gray of the sky barely stood out against the cold, wet gray of the canyon walls.

To their left, a tall, thin waterfall tumbled down over a series of large boulders that would have been easy enough to climb if dry. In the pouring rain, it made Jaela's heart sink.

"I can see a way up," Dralen hissed into her ear. "I'll go first and secure a rope if you want."

Jaela hesitated for a moment, then swallowed her pride and nodded, unshouldering her pack to dig out the rope. Dralen was ten times the climber she was, and he was taller, to boot. This was no time to play tough. She watched as he made his way up, one careful hand and foothold at a time. There was nothing especially challenging about it, except for maybe one flat rock that might be a little tall for her. But the rain pouring out of the sky and splattering across the rocks wasn't going to make it any easier. Dralen got to a ledge near the top, fiddled with the rope for a minute, then tossed it down. Jaela looped it around her waist, cinched it with a quick bowline knot, and started climbing.

The rocks were cold and slick, but the rope around her waist was reassuring. She took up the slack and re-secured it after every hold and only needed it once when her boot dislodged a loose bit of rock. She fell no more than two feet, the rope jerking against her hips but holding tight. Other than the near heart attack and the likely bruises, it did her no harm, and she was soon climbing again. She looked up at Dralen at every hold; his eyes shone with patient encouragement, despite the rain dribbling down from the brim of his hat. As he hauled her up onto the ledge, no more than ten feet from the surface, his eyes smiled, then grew serious, guiding her to look down.

Two cloaked figures stood on the path below, watching them with hard eyes beneath dripping hoods. Dralen pulled Jaela out of sight, and they leaned against the rock, soaked to the bone as rain gushed out of the sky and ran down the rock at their backs.

"At least they're not Logans," Jaela managed shakily. It was dark, or nearly so; it was hard to tell with the clouds, but there wasn't much daylight left at any rate.

"Let's just hope they don't come out for their nightly howls in the rain." He pulled up to the edge, glancing down and shaking his head. "They're gone," he said in a surprised whisper. "Let's get out of here and see if we can find some kind of shelter against this storm."

It wasn't much, but the overhang Dralen found kept the rain out. There was no flat place to lay down, so they huddled together as best they could on the rocky ground with only a thin blanket to cushion them and another to keep in their meager body heat. They both stank from the day's exertions, and Dralen's bony body wasn't much more comfort than the ground, but when she pressed her chest against his back, the chills subsided. She wondered if it did anything for him, having her pressed against him like this. Some boys and a lot of men looked at her in ways that made her want to kick them in the nuts, but Dralen never made her feel that way. Not by the way he looked at her, anyhow.

"I hope this isn't too awkward for you, Drale," she said after a while.

"Why would it be awkward, Jae?"

"I don't know. Boy and girl stuff, I guess. Anyway, I like girls, so." She felt her cheeks flush. She'd never actually said it out loud before. Not that it was a big deal; the Honey Girls at the mill lived together, but it wasn't exactly the norm.

"That's great, Jaela. Thanks for sharing. But either way, no, it's not awkward to share body heat when it's cold and rainy and you've spent the day sloshing through the canyons and climbing and you're so hungry you could eat your elbow and there's Logans about. It's just what friends do."

Jaela squeezed him tighter.

"I'm glad I joined you on your stupid little quest, Dralen."

7

The Logans came to Dralen in his dreams, hovering over him, waving their arms as if casting a spell. They did not tear him limb from limb or devour him with their yellow teeth, and their eyes were wild but oddly kind. He felt safe, protected, free somehow.

He awoke to an eerie predawn quiet. The rain had stopped, leaving a cool breeze in its place. Jaela's soft body provided ample warmth, and it was nice to be close to someone. Dralen hardly ever touched anyone except his Urpa, and he mostly liked it that way, but it was good to feel connected to the world sometimes. Except that he needed to pee, which meant peeling himself from Jaela's warmth.

She gave an annoyed little growl as Dralen crept off behind a shrub to relieve himself. He lifted the blanket and moved back in against Jaela, but she pulled away.

"Now I have to go. Thanks a lot."

She spooned him again when she returned, and they lay there half-awake as dawn painted the sky with streaks of pink and lavender, chasing the dark clouds in the distance. Dralen was used to seeing dawn like this by himself, but it felt different experiencing it with someone else. Not better or worse; just different. Like they had to share the sky, but also it belonged to both of them. And maybe they were both responsible for it somehow. Maybe he didn't have to carry its vast emptiness all on his own.

"We got any of that jerky left?" Jaela asked once they'd broken camp, such as it was.

"One fairly damp stick. What about the dried apples?"

"Couple slices, but they're probably wet and slimy by now."

"Sounds like a picnic."

It wasn't much to look at, but it tasted better than any meal Dralen had ever eaten. When they'd licked the last sticky bits from their fingers and washed it down with a few careful sips of water, Dralen looked Jaela in the eyes. He needed to know if she was still in this with him, after everything they'd seen. She returned his gaze with heat, almost a challenge in her eyes.

"I'd understand if you wanted to head back now, and I'd go with you."

"Fuck you, Dralen. We're going back in." Her finger hung in the air near his chest but did not touch it. He looked down at it, then back up into her eyes, which softened as her finger fell. "Don't you want to know what happened to Them?"

Dralen nodded, closing his eyes for a moment.

"You do have a plan, right?"

He nodded again, biting his lip against the grin that threatened to break out.

"I'm going to hate it, aren't I?"

If Jaela hated it, she kept her mouth shut about it. The canyons higher up the mountain were narrower, which made climbing easier. They hardly even needed the rope, but he dutifully attached it and moved it down for her as needed. She was plenty strong, but her confidence was for shit, and her fear kept her from reaching some holds she was capable of making. She kept it together, and in short order, they stood on the muddy path next to the rain-swollen creek. The footing looked tenuous in spots, but if the fisherfolk could move through, so could they.

He motioned to Jaela to stay put while he scouted ahead for tracks. Fortunately, the creek hadn't overflowed the path, and it didn't take long before he made out a bootprint that could only have been Theirs. Well, he supposed it could have been anyone with a hard-soled boot, but he didn't imagine the canyon dwellers got a lot of visitors. He wondered how They had managed to avoid detection; perhaps They were as skilled at stealth as They were with Their sword and bow. They might be a seasoned military scout or spy, trained for this type of mission. But his gut told him it was something else. Whatever their training, this was a solo trip. This was personal.

"Find anything?"

Dralen almost jumped at Jaela's voice in his ear.

"Dragon's guts, Jaela!" he hissed, angry at first until he saw her infectious smile.

"I'm getting better at this, aren't I?"

"I'm glad you joined me on my 'stupid little quest,' Jaela." He winked away her blush and nodded toward the path ahead. "They went this way. Canyons only extend another couple of miles, and there aren't as many footprints here, so maybe we're getting close."

The path hewed along the natural walls and was often slippery with the spray from the creek, which careened through the irregular patches of sandstone and granite. The roar of water ahead grew louder, and the mist filling the air was a little warmer as they reached a turbulent pool covered in sturdy wicker caging. The creek flowing into the pool was channeled by rows of boulders on either side, and it ran fast and furious down a set of rock stairs, which slowed its descent. Wicker cages with reedy mesh on the sides surrounded the outflow, where the water released gently before picking up speed as it poured down the rocks into the canyon below.

As they entered the chamber with the cages, they saw a narrow waterfall pouring a steady torrent of water fifty feet or more down onto the stairs. Next to the waterfall was a set of generous handholds chiseled into the rock, leading straight up along the side of the falls. A knotted rope dangled next to the handholds, soaked and mossy but thick enough to at least inspire some confidence.

"I don't know, Dralen. I don't know about that one."

"It's got handholds *and* a rope, Jae. What more could you ask for?"

She shook her head, staring into the water of the pool, her brows furrowing. Dralen looked too, and though the light was dim from the narrow window of sky above and it was hard to see clearly because of the cage, there seemed to be hundreds, or even thousands of creatures moving around in the water. As the light shimmered and flashed, he caught a closer look at them.

"Pinchies!" Jaela exclaimed.

"That would explain the cages and the mesh." He stared up at the waterfall, feeling the faint warmth of the mist. "Water's warmer here. Must be another hot spring feeding in somewhere above. I guess they eat whatever washes over this and gets battered on the stairs, and they just live in this pool until the canyon dwellers harvest them. The holes in the cages are small enough to keep out slinks and the like."

"And the mesh keeps the pinchies from getting washed downstream."

"I bet they check on them regularly, though. We'd better get a move on." He scanned the ground at the base of the cliff in the low light from the scattered sun bouncing off the canyon walls. It was too trampled to make out hard bootprints from soft, but They had been here. He was as sure of it as he was that the sun would set tonight and rise tomorrow. He gave the rope a tug; it was slimy with moss but felt solid, and the knots were big enough to grab hold of easily. He turned to Jaela, who stood rooted in place, arms across her chest.

"I'll go first and let you know what I see up there," he offered.

"Fuck that. I'm going first, and you go right behind me in case I start to panic."

"You're not going to panic, Jae. The handholds are six inches deep, and there's this big rope, see?" He grabbed it for emphasis. "You got this."

Jaela's eyes softened a little bit, and she took a deep breath and let it out as she started to climb. She was strong, and as long as she didn't panic, she'd be fine. She powered up the cliff, one steady hold at a time. She took a break about halfway up, breathing loudly.

"I'm fine, I'm just...taking a moment."

"You take all the time you need, Jae," he said in his gentlest voice. Sweat pooled under his arms and ran down his ribs as he tried to think of what he'd do if she started to panic for real. The thought sent him into a bit of a panic himself until Jaela sighed and started climbing again. He noticed her breath growing shallow as she reached the top, and her boot scrabbled on the last hold, sending grit into his eye. He squinted, watching as she hoisted herself up. Dralen soon joined her, breathing heavily. She shot him a panicked look and yanked him down behind one of the boulders making up the dam.

In the moment before his face hit the gravel, he saw another lake like the one they'd seen the day before, with another dozen or more fisherfolk working nets and cages. But something else caught his eye as well. A dark tunnel led out of the side of the canyon, which otherwise continued past the lake much as he would have expected.

"Shit, Dralen!" Jaela hissed. "We're lucky they didn't see us coming up. I doubt if we could sneak back down without being seen, and we sure as shit can't walk past them without they notice us!"

Dralen peeked over the edge of the boulder for a moment. The path along the side of the lake was in full view of the fisherfolk, with no cover at all. He studied the boulders making up the dam; there was a space behind the one they were using as cover they might be able to squeeze into. He glanced up at the ceiling, where a thick shaft of sunlight poured into the center of the chamber, illuminating part of the lake. It would be mid-afternoon by now, he guessed.

"What?" Jaela whispered, her face bright with curiosity.

"Remember how you hated my last plan?"

8

Jaela had to hand it to him. When Dralen came up with a bad plan, he took no half-measures. They waited in the cramped space between the rocks, Dralen's bony butt and elbows poking into her no matter which way they turned, until the light from the ribbon of sky above finally dimmed. The fisherfolk filed down the cliff, talking and laughing quietly. Jaela didn't dare to look, for fear they would see her eyes peeking between the rocks, but Dralen hurried over to the edge once the sound of their voices had faded. Jaela crept up beside him but didn't peer over the edge.

"They're scooping some of the pinchies up and…sorting them." She could barely hear his whisper above the roar of the falls. "Putting the big ones in a sack and tossing the little ones back…and now they're leaving." He turned to her, his eyes glowing in the shadows. Jaela's stomach twisted with hunger as she thought of the taste of steamed pinchies dusted with spice and served with steaming buttered new potatoes you got to eat with your fingers.

"You think they'd mind if we borrowed a few?"

She couldn't see much of Dralen's expression, but his silence was cutting.

"I'm sorry I'm a human who needs to eat, Drale," she hissed, suddenly flushed with anger.

"I know, Jae, I'm hungry too, but we can't—we can't risk stealing from them. We've already risked enough just being here."

"Yeah, and whose idea was that, anyway? Going into the canyons following after this mysterious stranger is one thing—a stupid thing, to be clear, but I was on board with that. But now that we know this is clearly their home, their land, their territory or whatever, maybe it's time we thank our lucky stars we haven't been caught yet and get out while we can!" Jaela had let her voice rise a little bit, and Dralen grabbed her wrist and pulled her in close, hissing in her face.

"Are you trying to get us caught?"

Jaela breathed deeply through her nose, glancing down at Dralen's hand, which released her wrist slowly. She was tempted to punch him in his stupid mouth for putting a hand on her like that, but he wasn't wrong about her being too loud. She was just so hungry and angry all at the same time. There should be a word for that.

"Sorry," he whispered, as if out of breath. "I just...there was no sign, no monument or statue, nothing like that. A village or a settlement has to have a marker telling you, 'This is our territory, you are guests in this land.' Like the rock pyramid back in Graueck. Or the plaque on the tree in Niehugg."

"You've really been thinking about this a lot." Jaela's anger rose up again, but it was tempered by curiosity at just how far up his own ass Dralen was at this moment. "You've got a whole explanation built up about how it's okay to go exploring through someone's territory just because they, what, didn't put up a sign?" She noticed her voice rising and lowered it again to a whisper.

Dralen didn't move or say a word for a long moment.

It was almost completely dark in the canyon now. The sliver of night sky visible left only the faintest shadows of the landscape below; Jaela saw Dralen as a black outline against the gloom. When he spoke again, his voice was low and careful.

"What do you want to do, Jaela? You're right; I'm hungry as hell and my guts are tied in knots. We won't last much longer if we don't get some food in us. But however dubious my position on trespassing on the fisherfolk's territory might be, I'm not stealing their food."

"You're the hunter, so if not pinchies or fish, what else could you catch us to eat?"

Dralen sighed into the darkness.

"I can't hunt at night, Jaela. But I promise, I'll climb up at dawn and find us something. Meantime, let's get moving to keep our minds off it, what do you say?"

Jaela sighed through her nose. Dralen's plan sucked, but it was better than standing here arguing with him while her stomach tried to eat her body from the inside out.

"I say light your candle and let's go for a swim."

The candle cast eerie shadows on the canyon walls Jaela was sure could be seen a long way off. They still hadn't found where the fisherfolk lived; it had to be somewhere between where they'd climbed up out of the canyon the night before and where they'd re-entered, unless there was a side passage they'd missed along the way. Dralen buttoned his pockets and motioned for Jaela to follow him. The water in the lake was clear, with only mild ripples from where the creek flowed into it. The ghostly silver shapes of sailbacks flashed by in the light from Dralen's candle, their sails occasionally brushing the surface. The edges of the lake were shallow, but as expected, the dam was the deepest part, and they'd have to swim unless they wanted to wade around the circumference of the lake. Even then, there was no guarantee there wouldn't be a part too deep to wade. They needed to get past the lake and into the cave mouth on the opposite side as quickly as possible so their light wouldn't be visible for long. Dralen waded in until the water was up to his chest, held the candle above the surface, and pushed off.

It was less than fifty feet to the shallows on the other side. Jaela followed as soon as it was clear he wasn't getting attacked by the fish or anything else. The water was cool, but not cold. It wasn't easy swimming in full clothes, boots, and a pack, but since Dralen hadn't stripped down, she went in fully dressed as well. Dralen seemed to move silently through the water, and Jaela made a lot more noise swimming than she would have liked, but if it bothered him, he'd just have to pound sand. They sat dripping on the other shore near the yawning cave mouth, listening, but heard no footsteps running toward them, no shouting voices. Only the sound of water running over the falls and the gentle murmur of the creek running into the lake to their right.

A trickle of water leaked out of the lake, forming puddles along the rough natural passage that wound away from the entrance. From the circle of light shed by the candle, it looked like this passage had been opened by tools, not water. Jaela knew the tales of mining in the canyons long ago, and how Dralen's great-uncle or something had died in a cave-in here. She wondered if the fisherfolk were miners too, or if they knew of the miners who lay buried somewhere beneath the rock.

Dralen stood, turning to face the passage, and Jaela stood next to him, shivering a little with her wet clothes clinging to her body. She didn't want to be out of arm's reach with nothing but a single candle between them and complete darkness. About ten feet in, the way was blocked by a waist-high wall of rubble with twin beams bisecting the passage like a giant X. Where they connected, words were burned into the wood:

Unstable area.

Do not enter.

Dralen moved forward, crouching to study the ground at the foot of the rubble. Jaela crouched with him, following his pointing finger, and saw it, plain as could be, in the light of his candle. A bootprint, hard like the ones he'd pointed out before. His fingers traced up the rocks, probably trying to guess where They would have stepped, and found another, just a heel, in the dust on a rock, and a third higher up.

"It's Them, isn't it," Jaela whispered.

Dralen nodded, gazing into the darkness ahead.

"Memory's mine," he murmured. Jaela cocked her head. "From the poem my Urpa told me. He said my great uncle Verg told it to him. The one who died here."

"Wait, *what?*" Jaela hissed. "You're saying your uncle—"

"Great uncle."

"Your great uncle who died in this mine told your Urpa a poem about the mysterious figure we're chasing after right now in this very mine?"

Dralen swayed, and sweat popped out on his brow. He put one hand on a rock, breathing slowly as his eyes grew distant. Jaela had seen him like this a couple of times, where he just kind of lost touch with the world for a little while. She took the candle from him, and he knelt down, pressing his forehead against the stone and closing his eyes. Jaela put the candle down and placed both hands on his shoulders, tentatively at first. He breathed out slowly, and she let her hands sink in, putting a little weight into him, just enough to anchor him. She wasn't sure what he needed, but his breathing steadied as she held still with him for a long moment.

Dralen's body jerked, and he sucked in a loud breath, gripping his ears with both hands as he fell back into Jaela's arms with a shiver.

"I've got you," she whispered, pressing him tight to her chest. Dralen let out a humming sigh, and Jaela loosened her grip a little, kissing the top of his head like a parent might do, if one had parents who believed in such gestures.

"Sorry, I—"

"Don't apologize for things that aren't your fault, Drale." She pinched the nerve between his neck and his shoulder, and he relaxed a little.

"Right, so—Thank you. I—They were here." He turned from her arms, staring at the bootprints and the corridor beyond. "I—I don't know how to say it, but...I *felt* Them. I *saw*

Them somehow, or a vision of Them, I don't know, it's probably just my imagination, but it seemed—"

"I told you it runs in the family, Drale. If you say you saw Them, I believe you. Tell me what you saw."

Dralen looked down, shaking his head. When his eyes met hers again, they were soft, hopeful. For the first time since they'd started this trip, it seemed like Dralen actually *believed*.

"They were here, Jae." His hands gripped her shoulders gently, pawing her muscles like a kitten making biscuits. "I...I think they still are." He released her shoulders, pointing down the passage. "They went that way."

9

Dralen moved slowly, as They had done in his vision, studying the ground, ceiling, and walls. Timbers fuzzy with mold propped the corridor in spots where it had been worked. He knew little of mining and less about underground construction, and none of it looked safe to him. He followed the bootprints, figuring if They had made it through, it was probably safe enough. It seemed the miners from long ago, whoever they were, had widened the natural caves in places to get through. A few side passages had been widened as well; Dralen cast a curious eye down some of them, but he'd already burned a quarter of his candle, and the bootprints were his only guide. It was cooler here, and Dralen rubbed his arms, to little avail; they'd have to keep moving or these wet clothes were going to become a problem.

As they approached an intersection, Dralen thought he heard voices. He snuffed out his candle, leaving them in complete darkness. He felt Jaela's heat as she moved close, felt her breath in his ear. A single plaintive note echoed in from the corridor ahead, lowering in almost musical scales to a deep, unnerving bass. A faint light appeared in the intersection, growing with each passing second. Dralen crouched behind a timber, and Jaela crouched next to him. Another voice joined the first, and they rose together, not in harmony exactly, but there was a kind of musical logic to their progression as if they were chasing the same sequence at different intervals. Dralen had heard music like this years ago at the Seventh Sun festival in Deep Cut Valley, performed by a row of long-bearded old men. It had made him feel uneasy as a child, and his chest tightened as their voices rose, intertwined, then fell again, ever approaching, ever louder. The light grew, though it was no brighter than a candle.

Jaela's hand touched his shoulder, and he leaned into her, feeling the tightness in his chest loosen just a little at her solidity. The voices grew louder still as they appeared in the intersection, two figures in robes like the others they'd seen, but their hair glittered in the candlelight as if interlaced with silver wires. One of them stopped, and his voice cut off suddenly. The other droned on for a moment before stopping as well, leaving them in eerie silence. Dralen looked down, knowing his eyes were the most visible part of him, hoping they couldn't make him and Jaela out at this distance. He heard them sniffing the air, no more than thirty feet away. They must have smelled the candle. Jaela's grip on his shoulder tightened, and he held his breath.

Low murmurs. The shuffling of feet. More sniffing. A sigh.

One voice rose again as they started moving, and the other soon joined in. Dralen let out a long, quiet sigh as Jaela released her grip on his shoulder and slid her hand around his neck, pulling him in for a hug.

"Dragon's guts, Dralen, that was close."

He squeezed her arm, holding onto her warmth for a moment longer, then slipped out of her embrace and stood. He listened for the voices, which had almost passed out of earshot, and for other sounds. Besides the distant rush of the creek, all was silent. He sparked the candle into life, studying the bootprints, which headed toward the intersection.

"Shall we?"

Jaela closed her eyes and flashed a tight smile. Even through her nervousness, her energy buoyed him. Whatever was to come, he was glad to be facing it with her.

The tracks led to the intersection, then disappeared in a mass of footprints leading both ways down the corridor, which looked to have been mostly human-made, perhaps blasted with blackpowder long ago and finished with hand tools. He couldn't imagine a space this size being carved out of the stone by sheer muscle and steel, but there were few lengths people wouldn't go to in order to get at the precious stones that lay beneath the earth. He knew the mine contained gemstones, mostly topaz, but it was rumored to have rarer stones as well, some with mystical properties, though no one could ever agree on what they might be. The presence of the Logans and the dangers of cave-ins had kept anyone from mining here in Dralen's lifetime, but the lines from Urpa's poem kept ringing in his head.

In search of treasures buried in memory's mine.

"So which way do we go?" Jaela whispered. At least she'd started being quiet now that they'd had a few close encounters.

"I might be able to make out Their tracks after a while, but there are so many footprints here, it's impossible to see anything." Dralen scuffed the grit on the floor with his boot. "I say we follow those two and see where they were going. If we go left, that's back toward the canyon. To the right seems more interesting." He became surer as he said it; They had gone right. He felt it in his bones.

"But if we go that way, and something comes at us from this direction, there's no way out."

"Fortune favors the mad, Jae."

Her face split into a grin, and she clapped him on the bicep much harder than he was expecting, knocking him sideways a step. She truly was stronger than most grown men, and he wondered if she forgot it sometimes.

They moved at a modest pace, slowly enough for Dralen to keep an eye on the tracks, on the off chance a bootprint jumped out at them, but it was dizzying to try to study them, and the cold, wet clothes were getting to him. The passage narrowed as it entered a natural area, which wound up and down, widened by human hands in a few spots. Little rivulets ran down the passage here and there, forming pools and even a still, shallow lake that stretched out of sight in a chamber so low they had to duck. They crossed on a set of evenly spaced flat stones that showed heavy traffic. He could see from the light of his candle that the water was no more than a few inches deep.

As the path rose past the water, he spotted it: a neat bootprint in the mud, mostly dried, a little to the side, so it hadn't been smushed by the many others. He briefly wondered if They had left it there on purpose for him to find. It seemed unlikely, but if they had the sight too, perhaps They somehow knew he was coming. He shook his head and pointed it out to Jaela, who nodded somberly.

As they crested the rise beyond the little lake, they heard footsteps hopping across the stones behind them. Jaela grabbed his arm, eyes wide with fear. Dralen pinched out his candle and clenched his jaw, trying to summon more calm than he felt. He scanned the shadowy corridor ahead, which twisted out of sight. If they ran, there was no telling what they'd be running into.

"Quick, but careful," he whispered. He started moving, and Jaela followed on his heels. He walked with his head cocked sideways, listening for the sound of voices or other activity ahead or behind. The corridor twisted this way and that, and a dim light appeared ahead, accompanied by low voices. A crevice led off to the left, though it appeared to peter out no more than twenty feet in. Dralen pulled Jaela into the crevice, feeling his way along the walls, which soon closed in on him.

"Get behind me," he hissed. He saw the shadow of Jaela's head shake as she uncoiled her bullwhip and crouched in front of him.

"Let's make real quiet and hope they don't notice us," she whispered as the light and voices of the newcomers approached. "But if they do, we blast past them and take off the way we came before they know what hit them."

Dralen opened his mouth to object, but the light was almost at the opening. The voices quieted as they approached, and two more figures stopped, dressed like the others, silver wires in their hair, and maybe something else as well, stones perhaps—Dralen didn't dare peer out too long between Jaela's ponytail and her shoulder. He hoped she was keeping her eyes closed as well.

Sniffing. Murmurs. The shuffling of feet. Words in an unfamiliar tongue, not overly loud, but commanding.

Directed at them.

Dralen opened his eyes as he felt Jaela stand up and step forward, holding her whip, which lay coiled on the floor.

"Anyone who doesn't want their face split in half better step out the way and let us pass." Her voice was strong through its tremble, raising every hair on Dralen's body. He slid to her left, fingering the sling on his belt as the whip twitched in her hand. The two figures pulled knives, staring at them with wide, uncertain eyes, but did not advance. Jaela took another step forward, and the two looked at each other, shifting on their feet and lowering to a crouch. Jaela's whip danced on the floor as she turned her head halfway toward Dralen.

"When I crack this, we run," she hissed out of the corner of her mouth.

He nodded, letting his fingers slide from his sling. It was no good in close quarters, and he'd need his hands free if they were going to make a break for it. His heart pounded in his throat, the muscles in his arms and legs twitching as Jaela's whip rolled into a series of elaborate curves, then shot out with a crack like a blackpowder explosion.

The two men staggered back, and Jaela burst forth like a charging ram with Dralen hot on her heels. One of the two men fell against the wall, but the other lunged for Jaela. She tucked into a half-slide, knocking his leg out from under him and elbowing his chest as she popped back up, a move he'd seen her use in the ring more than once. Dralen leapt over his flailing limbs and skidded around the corner, following Jaela's thudding footsteps down the shadowy corridor. They descended toward the lake in near darkness, but lights shone on the water as they made their way across the stepping stones. Two candles approached, with four more of the robed figures, who stopped their eerie chanting and ran down the hill toward them. Shouts and pounding footsteps sounded from behind them, and the two men from before soon stood on the other side of the water, faces red with exertion and anger.

Jaela fixed Dralen with fiery hard eyes, then turned to the four facing them, coiling her whip and adjusting her stance as if to strike.

"We just gotta get past them and we're home free."

"Jae," Dralen said softly, holding out a hand toward her.

"What?" She snarled without looking back at him.

"There's six of them, all adults. We're not fighting our way out of this."

She whirled around, eyes wide and furious, slipping off the stone and sending water splashing to the edges of the lake, where the six canyon dwellers watched with what looked like growing curiosity.

"Not with that shitty attitude we're not!"

Dralen swallowed, feeling a little cowed by her, but a giggle welled up inside him. Maybe he was delirious with hunger, fatigue, and cold, but the thought of Jaela going foot to foot with six grown men was both heart-warming and hilarious at the same time.

"Maybe we don't have to," he said, feeling a smile creep across his face. Jaela's expression softened a bit, and her whip hand lowered.

"Oh great, another one of your plans." She waved the coiled whip toward the four facing them, then toward the other two. "Why don't you share it with the whole class?" Her voice boomed, echoing off the low ceiling

"Maybe..." Dralen stepped forward, studying the faces of the four. One of them seemed to be listening to their conversation more intently than the others. Not a man, after all, he realized, or at least he didn't think so. But whoever they were, understanding flashed in their eyes.

"Maybe we can admit that we've made a big mistake," Dralen said in a loud voice, "that we're lost and starving and exhausted and in over our heads. Maybe we can tell them why we're here and ask for their help."

A smile grew on their face. They said a few words in their language and waved for the others to stand down. Everyone belted their knives, and Jaela slowly looped her whip back on her belt, eyeing the canyon dwellers and Dralen warily.

"I think you've come looking for someone." The woman's voice, for Dralen could tell the speaker was an older woman now, was scratchy, as if she smoked too much. "They're very busy right now, but why don't we get you a bite to eat and we'll see if They want to meet you when They're finished for the evening."

10

Jaela hunched beneath the heavy woolen cloak, poking at the stew with her spoon, teeth clenched as saliva ran in thick rivulets down her throat from the rich, fishy aroma. These people were too damned nice. It had to be a trick.

Dralen was plowing through his bowl, slurping and *mmm*ing. She sighed, sliding the spoon beneath a chunk of fish and a blob that looked like a dumpling. She looked up at the one who'd spoken to them, who watched Jaela with calm amusement in her eyes.

"I've already eaten, but I can take a bite of yours if that would make you feel more comfortable."

Jaela shook her head, maintaining eye contact as she raised the spoon to her mouth. Her eyes slammed shut as the flavors flooded her taste buds, fishy, salty, and rich, surely the best single bite of food she had ever put in her mouth. She opened her eyes as she swallowed, and she let her mouth twist into a half-smile in response to the old woman's grin.

"This stuff's amazing, right Jae?" Dralen spoke with one hand half-covering his mouth, which was still full of food. "Honestly, this is the best stew I've ever tasted, and that's no exaggeration." He held out his hand in appreciation. "We're mighty thankful, especially after..." His voice fell, and his hand followed.

"I'm sure you had your reasons. It took a lot of courage for you two to come all the way up here. The hill folk usually steer far clear of the canyons, especially since the cave-in." She shook her head, looking down. "Were you kin to the one who disappeared?"

Jaela studied Dralen, whose Adam's apple moved as he nodded.

"He was my great-uncle. I never knew him."

"But you know of..." She paused, staring into Dralen's eyes, then glancing at Jaela.

Dralen set down his bowl and ran his fingers through his hair, saying nothing. Jaela wondered if he was having one of his little moments.

"I don't know anything, not exactly. But I saw Them when I was out hunting the other day, not far from the lower entrance. Something about Them just stuck in my head. And then something my Urpa said just kind of...spoke to me. And I had to follow Them. I had to know."

The woman tented her fingers, nodding.

"Kay told us you would come."

A chill ran across Jaela's skin, standing all her little hairs on end.

"Kay," Dralen whispered.

"These things run in the family, as I understand it. What surprises me is that we knew of your coming, yet you made it all this way without being noticed. Only a few hundred feet more and you'd have found them all by yourselves. You truly are of one blood."

Footsteps approached outside the candlelit alcove where they were eating. Words were exchanged, and their host nodded and stood.

"Your clothes are dry. Once you've changed, we will take you to see Kay."

Jaela held Dralen's hand as they followed their host and a small group of the canyon dwellers through a series of passages back to the lake and the corridor beyond. As they passed the crevice where they'd hidden out before, their guide turned and put a finger over her lips.

"From here on, please be quiet until told to speak. Kay requires great concentration for their work."

The corridor led to a large room, what Jaela thought must be a mining gallery, half filled with a massive pile of rubble from what appeared to be an old cave-in. A swath near one wall had been cleared of rock, and the dim light grew brighter as they rounded the hill of rubble and stood facing the open space. Jaela's breath caught in her throat at the sight of the six figures seated in a circle, holding hands and chanting. Their matted hair was festooned with silver wires and glittering gems, and their gaunt faces and pained expressions were all too familiar, leaving no doubt in her mind who they were.

These were Logans.

She gripped Dralen's hand tighter, but he hardly seemed to notice. He stared at the person kneeling before a large flat stone in the center of the circle, their hands hovering over a black sphere the size of an apple that sat in a golden bowl. They wore a gray cloak and worn brown boots, and their close-cropped hair was adorned with the same wires as the Logans, but woven into an almost crown-like shape, with the gems pressed tight against their head. A single lantern on a rock behind them cast a thin light over the proceedings.

None of them seemed to notice the intrusion at first, but after a moment, the person in the center lifted their hands from the sphere and turned toward Dralen. Their wide pupils nearly swallowed the gray of their eyes, only slowly shrinking as their expression sharpened.

"You have come." They held out one hand in a gesture of beckoning.

Dralen nodded, slipping out of Jaela's grip and taking a step forward. Two of the Logans released their hands to let him pass, then closed the circle once he was inside. Jaela fingered her whip, and their guide shook her head faintly. She let her hand fall to her side. She knew it wouldn't do anything, but her stomach was tied in knots seeing Dralen surrounded by the Logans, who were all the creepier sitting still as statues. She was sure that any minute, they would leap up and begin their terrible howling, claws outstretched, teeth bared as they fell upon Dralen and tore him to pieces. She dared a look at their hands, which were not, as she had imagined, any different than the other fisherfolk. Nor were their clothes, or their faces, except for the contorted expressions that left their teeth unnaturally visible and their eyes bulging wide, huge black pupils swallowing their irises. Could it be the Logans were nothing more than members of this tribe who had—

"I'm Dralen." His low voice carried in the now-silent chamber. "And you are..."

"My name is Kay, but it was not always." They spoke with a Fenylbyr accent, though it had a whisper of the hills beneath it. Their cloak and boots were worn but of fine quality. City quality. Maybe even military quality. "You may have heard of me by a different name I no longer use. I am your first cousin once removed."

Jaela racked her brains to figure out who in the dragon's teats that might be. She was terrible with names and even worse with family trees. Kay looked to be in their fifties, and she thought she saw a faint family resemblance, but she could have been imagining it.

"Are you...my great uncle Verg's child?"

They paused, staring at Dralen for a long moment with eyes that burned Jaela even though she was not their target.

"The answer to that is rather complicated, and I prefer not to speak for those who are not present." They glanced toward Jaela, who wished she had Dralen's hand to hold as their gray eyes pierced hers. "Are you family?"

She shook her head as she tried to muster the courage to speak.

"Just a friend."

"Quite a friend you must be to follow Dralen all the way here. Either that or quite a fool."

A nervous giggle slipped out of Jaela's lips.

"I like to think a little of both."

A gentle smile formed on their lips, and they turned back to Dralen.

"What I have to share is personal, family business you may not even want to share with your parents. Are you sure—"

"Jaela's more family than my parents ever were." Dralen's voice was hard despite the tremor that crept in, and Jaela couldn't stop the tears that welled up at his words. "She can hear anything you've got to say."

"I'm not going to tell you anything," Kay said, gesturing toward the black globe. They removed their delicate crown of wires and stones and held it toward Dralen's head. "I'm going to show you."

11

Dralen swallowed hard to chase away the shadows from the edges of his vision as They slid the crown onto his head. Kay, he reminded himself. They had a name now; it felt almost disappointing somehow.

"My mother was like you," Kay said. "Like me. Sighted." They tapped their forehead. "Your Urpa too, I believe, but not your parents?"

Dralen shook his head.

"Not that I ever noticed. But I was never really sure until…" He paused. It wasn't exactly true, he realized. He'd always been sure, deep down. He'd just managed to convince himself otherwise, time and again, until whenever the feeling surfaced, he'd learned to dismiss it. "Until I saw you."

"That was no accident. I watched you hunt the nildeer. You're an extraordinary shot, even though you missed the mark by an inch. I'm not sure I could have done better with my bow, and I'm a trained royal scout."

Dralen's heart warmed at the compliment, and he realized that his vision had cleared. All his anxiety, all his dread, had vanished as Kay spoke to him in a voice that was suddenly familiar, though he'd never heard it before.

"And you watched me because…"

Kay gestured toward the orb, which was shiny and opaque, set in a bowl of gold stamped with ornate floral designs, the kind of thing one might see at a market in the Valley, a bauble for the idle rich meant to look like a magical item.

"My mother is dying. She may be dead already by now. I do not know. She never told me the story of how she got to Fenylbyr. How she came to be…herself. But I never stopped asking. One night, as I was nursing her after a long bought of coughing, she gave me this, along with a set of instructions, written in a code that took a week to decipher even with the key she gave me." They pointed to the crown on Dralen's head. "The stones on your head are called memory stones, a vein of which she found here while mining long ago but was unable to fully extract because of the cave-in that almost took her life."

Dralen's skin tingled, and his head buzzed with the implications.

"Almost?"

They nodded, fixing him with a knowing stare.

"This orb contains her memories, or those she chose to put in it. From that time, and some of what came before. I've been studying it for several days, with the help of the enlightened ones. She told me I could share these memories with you and your Urpa if he's still alive."

"He is." Dralen's eyes watered as he wondered for how long. "How does it work?"

Kay sighed, furrowing their brow.

"That's the hard part. It will take some time for you to find your way, as our minds all work differently. Perhaps, being younger, you will adapt more easily. Or it may take you longer. It's impossible to say." Kay held their hands over the orb as they had done before. "You hold your hands close to the orb and concentrate, and you should feel its pull, almost like a magnet. It can be overwhelming at first, but your mind is strong, and the enlightened ones will give you a boost. You will find your way."

Sweat dripped down Dralen's armpits, despite the chill in the air. He glanced around the circle of Logans, or enlightened ones, as Kay had called them. He could see now that they were no different than the other canyon dwellers, besides their facial expressions and their eyes, whose pupils were eerily huge, staring through him rather than at him. He looked at Jaela, who watched with wide, wet eyes. She blinked her encouragement, and he blinked back.

"Okay, I guess." He looked into Kay's eyes, which were cool but kind.

"I will be right here. If you get confused, just lift the crown from your head. There's no danger here. Only the chance to understand someone you never knew but who knew you, in a way."

Dralen stared at the sphere, which seemed to absorb all the light in the room. He could feel it calling to him, even though his hands were at his sides, like the warmth of a fire he was standing just a little too far from. He held out his hands, which hovered around the sphere, held in place as by a static charge. Shadows closed around the edges of his vision, but the darkness was comforting this time, inducing peace in place of panic. He closed his eyes and let it in.

Images flashed in his mind's eye, hundreds all at once, impossible to discern, spinning together like water flowing down a drain. He grew dizzy, and panic seeped in, but he heard Kay's voice in his head: *There's no danger here.* He shifted his awareness to his breathing, letting out a long, slow breath through his nose, then took in another deep one and returned to the vortex of images. He narrowed his focus, and the spinning slowed. He saw faces in candlelight, smiles, laughter around a table, and a baby clutched to a breast, suckling. His arm around the mother's shoulders, the baby's bright gray eyes staring up into his, searching. His heart warmed with an ache deeper and more beautiful than anything he'd ever known.

His mind was yanked out of the moment, dragged backward, as if tumbled upstream attached to a rope, bouncing off memories like mossy boulders. The jingle of a bell, a store full of customers, sweat and bustle and heaving of heavy sacks. More tumbling, spinning, confusion. An empty room with dusty shelves and broken windows, full of promise. A woman whose eyes were hard with experience but soft with understanding. A kiss, strange and bewildering but also wonderful, rife with soft, squishy, forbidden feelings.

A long journey full of loneliness, hunger, and dread. Scowls and mistrust from villagers mixed with a few kind faces, bits of food, and offers of shelter. Everything hurt; her back especially, where it had been twisted beneath the rubble, her broken right hand, and her knee. It had gotten dislocated again during her journey and was popped back into place by a laconic shepherd who'd found her in agony, starving and parched on a sun-baked hillside. The shepherd hadn't said a word to her other than 'Hold still,' but he'd helped her back to her feet and given her water and a stick to hobble with, and his dour face was etched into her memory.

The gleam of the stones revealed by her pick, dull yellow in the light of her lamp. As her fingertips brushed against them, she'd known without knowing—it had taken her years to find out exactly what they were, but she'd known she couldn't tell a soul. She'd worked at them in secret in spare moments once she'd found enough topaz to be worth the trip, but it was tedious, tricky work, as the other miners were always about, and she couldn't risk them finding out. And then one day, some fool had brought blackpowder to expose a topaz seam he swore was the motherlode, and it had all come crashing down.

The boom had echoed in, shaking the ground, and she'd darted out of the way as a chunk of ceiling dropped right where she'd been working. She'd run for the exit as fast as she could, but a passage had collapsed on top of her as she'd almost reached the canyon. She heard the cries of the other miners, some trapped, others trying to rescue them. She called out for help for a while, but her voice grew weak and the sounds of the rescuers faint. As she realized the mine had settled and she could extricate herself, a plan formed in her mind.

The village would never accept her as she was, never give her a chance to try. Even the man they saw her as was too frivolous, too carefree for Graueck. Living as herself there was impossible. But in Fenylbyr, she'd heard people lived as they pleased. Women living as men, men as women, the villagers would say, voices dripping with scorn. Vera had always been careful not to smile when the topic came up, not on the outside anyway. But she'd always dreamt of finding her way there and seeing if it was really true.

And so, she waited, letting their calls go unanswered, wriggling and wrenching herself free one agonizing inch at a time. Their calls finally stopped, and she knew it must be near nightfall. They would be heading back, fearful of a legend whose reality she knew to be all too benign. Her lamp had gone out, leaving her in silent darkness, but she knew every inch of these tunnels and the canyons beyond. She had nothing to fear. She wriggled out from beneath the slab of rock that pinned her, though she had to dislocate her knee in the process. Her cries must have summoned the enlightened ones, for they soon appeared with their candles, pupils wide, faces drawn with concern.

They did not speak in this state, but they helped her up, murmuring their repetitive syllables. When they were inside the canyons, their voices were low, their movements controlled; only when they went out for their dancing runs did their voices rise in the way that had inspired the legends. The meditative state was brought on by a fungal tea, she'd learned, part of a ritual performed at each quarter-moon by a small group of the canyon dwellers. Something about helping the moon travel across the sky if she understood their language correctly. She'd been learning from them every chance she got, but there was never enough time. And in her current state, even less.

They wrapped her knee in tight bandages and helped her back to the canyon, to the path she knew well. She bowed in thanks, speaking a few words in their tongue, which they seemed to understand, though they responded only in a series of rapid blinks. They waved awkwardly, then hurried away in the direction of the upper canyons, no doubt to sing the moon across the skies once again.

She hobbled to the lower canyon entrance, her body a mosaic of pain, but her heart full with the promise of freedom. Her boy Kinnin was nearly grown; at fifteen, he didn't need her anymore, didn't want to have much to do with her anyway. Her wife shied away from her touch, and Vera respected her wishes, painful as it was to see her jump whenever Vera approached. Whatever spark had once flared between them was long cold. Her family might not be better off without her, but they would survive. The cache of topaz she'd left in her drawer would make sure of that.

Ahead, she saw the valley road alongside the gurgling stream. The path back to the village ran off to the left of the stream; to the right, a small trail led over a hill and out of sight, in the direction of Fenylbyr.

The quarter-moon was just rising over Fishback Ridge, ghostly silver and pocked with what she'd always imagined to be lakes filled with clear, dark water, with no one around to see, no one to hide from. She'd long dreamt of stripping down on the rocky shores of those lakes, peeling away her flesh suit to reveal the shining skin beneath, the natural curves no one could see but her. The rocks would be sharp beneath her feet, the water clear and black and bottomless. She'd take a deep breath of the universe, then dive in, letting the endless dark infinity pull her into its embrace.

She shuffled along the path beside the creek. She felt her age in a way she never had before. Her hand was broken, her back hunched with pain, and her knee wobbled with every step. But as she turned to the right, a lightness grew in her heart. The moon was only a quarter full. She had all the time in the world to help chase it across the sky.

Dralen lifted the crown from his head slowly, keeping his eyes closed for a moment as the world came rushing back in. The low chants of the Logans were soothing now, and he realized he'd heard them in the background the entire time he'd been...inside her memories? He glanced up at Kay, who studied him, an inscrutable expression in their eyes.

"She's...she's my great-aunt?"

Kay smiled. "Her name is Vera, and she would have liked to meet you, but this will have to do."

Dralen paused, wondering what to tell Urpa. All these years he'd thought his brother was killed in a mine, but it turned out he never had a brother, and his sister was dying, or maybe dead, in a city far away. And her child, whom Urpa had known as his nephew Kinnin, was not a nephew at all, but...was there a word for what Kay was to Urpa? He supposed it didn't matter what you called someone, as long as you saw them for who they were. Which, Dralen realized, was a person no doubt deep in grief at their loss.

"I'm so sorry," he said. "She seems like a wonderful person."

"She is." They put a hand on his shoulder, tentative at first, then firmer as Dralen leaned in. "When I left Graueck, I knew in my heart she was still alive. Like you, I skulked about the canyons for a bit, looking for clues, but my heart told me to go west. I joined the service, wound up in Fenylbyr, and kept looking..." They sighed, shaking their head. "I was as surprised as you might imagine when I finally found her. I was angry, I was confused, but when she took me in her arms, something inside me just...melted." Kay stopped, covering their eyes with their hand. Dralen saw tears leak down their cheek, sparking his own, which he fought the urge to stifle. They flowed nonetheless, and he made no move to stop them. Kay sniffed, wiping their eyes, and Dralen did the same.

"I never knew her full story until she shared the stone with me."

"Was it hard for her? In Fenylbyr? To live...as herself?" Dralen's ears burned, but he sensed it was okay to ask. Such a life would never have been possible in Graueck.

"If it was, she never spoke of it. She didn't like to talk about the past, or of unpleasant things. It must have been hard back then; even now, things could be better. She certainly made it easier for me though. I gather life in the village is still much as it was?"

Dralen snorted.

"I can only speak for the last fifteen or so years, but I don't get the impression a whole lot has changed. They still want to keep everyone in boxes."

"And yet here you are."

Dralen searched Kay's eyes, which he now saw were not gray but light blue, flecked with shards of green to give a grayish effect. They seemed to see through him, but not in a piercing way; they connected with his, sharing a vision of him that Dralen himself was blind to. A lone figure in the hills, silhouetted against the rising moon, gray eyes gleaming from beneath their hood. Not a boy or a girl, a man or a woman; a person. Just as Dralen saw Kay.

Kay's gaze did not falter. Dralen looked down, but still, he could feel their eyes fixed on him, asking the silent question. He could always choose not to answer; it was his business, after all, and if he hadn't shared with Jaela before now, why would he share it with a total stranger who just happened to be a distant relative? But as he looked back up into their eyes, he saw the soft light of understanding, and something broke inside him, a wall he'd been keeping up for so long he'd forgotten it was even there. All the days and nights spent alone in the hills, chasing down nildeer and murmuts, setting traps, had been a distraction.

As long as he was away from the village, away from people, he didn't have to think about how absurd their world seemed to him, the way they divided and sorted people like tools on a shelf. Only there was never a shelf that fit him, never a peg to hold his particular shape. Men and women, girls and boys, acting the way folks always had, expecting things from each other because of the bodies they were born in. None of it made any sense. It was easier just to hide away in the hills.

To his mother, he would always be too much or not enough like his father, too hard or too soft, but never enough. Never enough.

To everyone else, he was just a weird boy who'd grow up to be a weird man no woman would want to be with. Which suited him just fine, since he had no interest in such things, and people could think of him as they liked. The less he had to do with them, the better. There were always a few who didn't care, who saw him for more than what use he could be, like Jaela, Urpa, or the Bee Girls. But to the rest of Graueck, Dralen would never be anything but a disappointment. And the feeling was definitely mutual.

Now that he had met Kay, now that he had seen the life Vera had lived, there was no putting himself back in that box.

"What will you do, now that you know?" Kay's soft voice stirred Dralen from his reverie.

"About Vera?"

"What else?"

Dralen's ears burned at the gentle warmth of the question, but he pushed it down.

"I'll tell my Urpa, I guess. It's his sister, after all. He can keep a secret." He drummed his fingers against his knee. "This is a secret, right?"

"I leave that up to you. Mother—Vera said you could tell whomever you trusted. If you think the village is ready to know, you can figure out the best way to tell them. Although if I were you..." They pointed toward Dralen's chest. "I'd ask if your mother is ready to know who *you* are. Who knows? She might surprise you."

Dralen nodded, sudden tears rising behind his eyes and flooding down his face. Kay spread their arms wide, and he relaxed into their gentle strength until he'd cried himself dry. It didn't take long; years of training had kept him from expressing his emotions too freely, but he shed more tears than he had in quite a while.

He turned to Jaela, whose eyes were as wet as his, and the Logans silently released their arms to let him through. She wrapped him in a much tighter and fiercer hug than Kay, and he clung to her, struggling to draw breath as she lifted him off the ground, then finally set him down, patting him on the shoulders.

"Did you find out what you came here for, Drale?"

He let his forehead lean against hers, pressing his hands against the back of her head.

"So much more, Jaela. Thank you for joining me on my stupid quest."

She pulled back, a wide smile beaming out of her red, tear-splotched face.

"Thanks for having me, buddy."

Their goodbyes were brief, as he'd known they would be. Kay gifted them with a small bag of stones, which they assured Dralen would be worth a small fortune if sold with care.

"Vera wanted me to give you a leg up, given the challenges you may face."

Dralen reddened at the thought; he wasn't sure what those challenges might be, but the stones would make it easier to face his mother, knowing he didn't need her support to survive. It wasn't like she was going to kick him out, but the thought of sitting her down and talking to her was more than he could bear. They never really talked about anything, let alone about...whatever this was.

Maybe Kay was right. Maybe she'd understand if he just gave her a chance. As he pictured the perpetual worry lines on her face, he wasn't so sure. But if he could venture into the canyons following a mysterious cloaked figure and stand in a circle of Logans, surely, he could tell his mother who he really was. Just as soon as he figured that out.

Maybe in the meantime, he could start by telling her who he wasn't.

The canyon dwellers escorted them to the lower entrance and gifted them with some fish jerky and hard biscuits, which kept them nourished until Dralen shot a nice fat murmut that evening in the marsh where they collected the hushweed for Urpa's medicine. They cackled and gestured wildly next to their little fire as they retold moments from their adventure, watching the murmut sputter and crisp. Dralen's spice mix had gotten wet, but he'd managed to scrape enough onto the skin to bring out the flavor, and it was the second-best meal he'd had in recent memory, after the fish stew in the canyons.

Jaela licked the grease from her fingers, reflections of the flames dancing in her glassy eyes.

"We did it, Dralen. We fucking did it." Her voice was subdued but rich with the warmth of accomplishment.

"We did at that."

"Our parents are gonna be *so* pissed."

"Your sister too, I expect."

"Ugh. I'm going to have to be nice to her for, like, a year."

"Would it be such a bad thing?" Dralen winced as he said it, but the way Jaela had slammed her sister against the woodpile had stuck in his mind like a tick's head lodged beneath the skin. She turned to him, her jaw set like she was going to spit, then she sighed.

"You're right. Fuck!" She ran her hand down her face, jaw pushed out in anger. "Just because my parents treat me like shit doesn't mean I have to pass it on."

Dralen scooted closer, putting a tentative arm around Jaela's shoulder. She leaned her head against his, and he had to brace himself as her weight settled into him.

"You're doing great, Jae. Ain't none of us perfect."

She squeezed his knee and settled in further. He leaned against her, finding the right balance, and they sat as one lump of flesh watching the fire melt away in the cool mountain dark.

12

Jaela braced herself for a slap as she approached her mother, who was washing her hands after a morning of pressing cheese. She deserved it for running off like that, but it was going to be hard to just stand there and take it.

Her mother turned halfway, as if she'd recognized Jaela's step, then swirled around and launched into her arms, clutching her with a fierceness Jaela hadn't known she possessed.

"Oh, dear sweet Jaela, we thought we'd lost you!" She pushed Jaela to arm's length, studying her with hard, teary eyes.

"I'm fine, Mami, and I'm so, so sorry I left off like that." She looked down, then back up. She'd promised herself she would face this like an adult. "You got my note?"

Her mother nodded, tears streaming down the lines on her face.

"We got sidetracked, but we made it through all right. We're fine. Everything's fine. How are the littles?"

Her mother barked a laugh, wiping her nose.

"Georgi acts like she runs the place. I think she likes playing big sister. I might let her be in charge of you for the next week or two, after that stunt you pulled." She turned and picked up a towel to dry her hands, then patted her face, which had regained some of its hard lines.

"I'm gonna be extra nice to her. I swear."

"I guess it wouldn't hurt." She reached for Jaela's face, which she hadn't done since Jaela was a child, then stopped. Jaela took her wrist and pulled her hand against her cheek, letting her tears flow at the warmth of her mother's palm, the closeness they'd lost over the years.

Though the touch lasted only a few seconds, Jaela's cheek felt warm for the rest of the day as her mother filled her with food and drink, helped draw her a bath, and laid out clean clothes for her. She heard her siblings giggling outside the bathroom door as she dressed, and she wiped the steam from the mirror and took a long look before going out to greet them. It would be hard stepping back into the mixture of chaos and tedium that had always been her life, but the face she saw staring back at her looked older somehow, though it had only been a few days. She'd be sixteen soon, and it was time she stopped whinging about the life she had and started thinking about the life she wanted.

"Jae, you almost done in there?" Georgi whined.

"Just drying my hair!"

She already knew what she didn't want—to settle down with some stupid boy and make cheese or herd cows. Though she supposed she could settle down with a girl instead, like the Bee Girls, she would still prefer a life that didn't involve food-related pursuits. She had some capital now, thanks to the stones Kay had given them; she could use them to start her own affair, though she couldn't liquidate them until she turned sixteen. But where would she even begin? Other than being big, strong, and good at foot-fighting, she didn't know how to do much besides work with cows or cheese.

"Jae! Mami said you'd help get the stove going. I'm not allowed—"

"I SAID—" Jaela took a breath, then lowered her voice. "I'll be right out."

She ran the towel through her hair one more time, tying it in a wet ponytail. The comb dropped from the basin, and she caught it with her foot, then flipped it back up with a fluid motion, smiling with satisfaction. If memory served, there would be a foot-fighting open tournament tomorrow night at dusk. She hadn't competed in an open since last year, but she'd made it to the second round and only lost on a technicality. She was a year older and an inch taller now, not to mention heavier and stronger. The pot was fifty rabble for first place, twenty for second, and ten for third. She'd heard they had tournaments in the Valley with pots in the thousands, where the fighters wore elaborate costumes and even had fans who dressed like them.

She shook her head, smiling at the absurdity of it, but her smile never faded. Even as she opened the door and the littles came spilling in, climbing all over her, talking all at once, asking where she went, why she was gone so long, did she find the magic herbs she was looking for, was Dralen her boyfriend, did they make a baby, and a hundred other questions that had her cackling with delight. She picked them all up, the youngest two on her shoulders squealing and giggling and Georgi under her arm howling in protest, and squeezed through the door and out into the yard.

"Bats and Logans, and you lot are all bats!"

Jaela's arms shot to the sides, her hands extending into claws, her eyes wide and wild as she bared her teeth. Her siblings' squeals rose high and shrill as they wheeled about like chickens fleeing a fox and disappeared into the village.

She turned to see her mother standing in the doorway, hands on her hips, a wry smile on her face. Jaela flashed her a grin, then shuffled off behind the henhouse, moaning and wailing, following the gleeful giggles of the littles, and several other children who had apparently joined in the game. Though she was far too old for such childish pursuits, she felt a solemn duty now to preserve the legend of the Logans, so that the children of the village would grow up knowing in their hearts that under no circumstances should they ever go near the canyons.

Especially not at night.

13

Dralen's mother poured the brandy slowly into three of the elegant pear-shaped glasses she kept on the top shelf, careful not to spill a drop. The brandy had been a wedding present, twenty years old at the time, which would make it almost forty now, though Dralen didn't know if aging counted after the bottle had been opened. He'd only seen her drink it once, at his father's wake when he was four. It was just about the only thing he remembered from that time, or of his father. That and falling on a hike and his father rubbing his scraped knee better, sunlight blinding him to the face he'd long imagined but could only see in his dreams.

She set the glasses in front of Dralen and Urpa, who studied Dralen with warm, attentive eyes. Knowing eyes, Dralen thought briefly as his hand instinctively raised his glass in time with his mother and Urpa.

"To a straight path leading ever gently downhill." Her eyes crinkled in a smile as she sniffed, then tilted the honey-brown liquid slowly back.

Dralen did the same, wincing pre-emptively, but the bite of the brandy was offset by a subtle sweetness, unlike the harsh whiskey he nipped out of Jaela's flask now and then. Warmth spread through his chest and head, flushing his cheeks and bringing unexpected dampness to his eyes.

"It's probably only going to be a few weeks, Ma."

"Don't count your Jaela out so easily." Urpa shook his finger at Dralen. "I heard there's not a man in the village who'll face her after the humbling she put on Big Jordo."

"This is the Valley, though. There's people there who foot-fight for a living."

"Mind you don't talk to Jaela like that," his mother scolded. "She'll take her cues from you."

"Jae never listens to a word I say, Ma." Dralen chuckled softly into his brandy, then took another sip, hoping the fire of the liquor would bring him the courage to give word to his jumbled thoughts.

"I daresay she does more'n you think." Urpa put a hand on Dralen's. His fingers were soft and warm, comforting. "A lot of folk would listen to you if you'd just open your mouth once in a while and say what's on your mind."

Sweat popped out over Dralen's forehead, on the back of his neck, and under his arms. He took a sloppy sip of his brandy and wiped his mouth, then the tears that had leaked from his eyes without his having noticed. He laughed weakly as his mother's hand crept across the table. He let her take his, gripping her fingers, sniffing because he had no hands free to wipe his nose.

"I guess before I go, I should tell you what really happened in the canyons. What I discovered. Who I met."

Urpa's hand pulled back, and he packed his pipe and lit it, eyeing Dralen with deep curiosity.

"Is this something to do with Verg?"

Dralen nodded, running his finger around the impossibly thin rim of the glass, so fine it was almost sharp. How could he even begin?

"Yes and no. But it's also something to do with me."

His mother took a long sip of her brandy, still clutching his hand tight, and urged him on with deep, understanding eyes.

Epilogue

Dralen kneaded Jaela's thick trapezoids, which were rock-hard with tension. The Sun Bowl was more than half-full, with over a thousand people filling the lower deck and scattered around the balcony, their voices a buzzing drone. Jaela sat like a statue, elbows and knees wide, staring down her opponent, a man half a head taller than her with the knotted physique of a boxer. Dralen had watched his previous matches; he was faster than Jaela, probably stronger in the upper body, and had years more competition experience. On paper, she didn't stand a chance.

"Just keep your mind soft, Jae. He's a stiffie. You won't beat him on strength or speed or technique."

"Well, that's reassuring." She half-turned her head, the corner of her mouth turning up in a smile.

"I didn't say you won't beat him. Just look at his eyes." Dralen pointed to the man, who called himself The Broom. He wore a tan outfit with rushes tied around his ankles and an atrocious thick mustache to complete the look. He glared at Jaela, teeth gritted in a sneer. "He's intimidated by you. Doesn't want to get beat by a girl."

"I'm not a girl. I'm a woman," Jaela growled under her breath, her muscles tensing beneath his fingers.

"I don't know that Mr. Broom over there sees it that way. If you beat him, he got beat by a girl, and he'd never live it down. So, he'll come at you hard, try to make it look like you have no place in this ring. Like you should have just stayed at home playing with your dollies."

Jaela sprang up, kicking over the stool and spinning to face Dralen. Her eyes bulged out of her bright red face as she gripped his shoulders, squeezing so hard he gasped. The bell rang, and Jaela flashed a quick smile.

"Thank you," she whispered, then spun back around and danced to the edge of the ring in that weird side-stepping motion she had, shifting from one powerful haunch to the other, her thick arms rolling loosely to either side. The yellow and black striped shirt the Honey Girls had made for her clung tight around her form, which would make it harder for an opponent to grab hold of her. It also brought home just how strong and grown-up and beautiful she was. He scanned the crowd and noticed a rather large number of girls in attendance with yellow and black stripes painted on their faces, buzzing in unison as Jaela entered the ring. Dralen's heart swelled with pride.

The Broom marched forward stiffly, spread his legs wide, and cocked his arms like a pinchie preparing to defend itself. He was a formidable opponent who had fought semi-professionally for several years. He knew exactly what he was doing. Jaela was probably going to lose. But that hadn't stopped Dralen from placing a thousand rabble bet on her.

The announcer finished his spiel, and the bell rang.

Jaela and The Broom circled and closed, circled and closed, testing each other with a few feints before The Broom came in with a furious set of slide-kicks that sent Jaela scrambling backward, almost losing her balance out of the ring. She pinwheeled out of the way and they began circling again. Seconds later, The Broom launched a barrage of shin sweeps, but Jaela danced out of the way, and on the last one managed to lift her leg beneath his, upending him. As his leg lifted above waist level, she was on him like lightning, cracking him in the chest with an elbow that sent him crashing to the ground, coughing and clutching his chest.

The crowd roared, and Jaela crouched near her fallen opponent, holding out a hand to offer help, but he slapped it away and scrambled to his feet, still clutching his chest for a moment. The crowd booed at his antics, and he waved them off, and the referee as well as he crouched again, legs wide and arms set like claws. Jaela closed on him quickly, coming in hard with her knees, which he blocked with his hands at first, then his thighs as her punishing blows kept coming and he couldn't muster a counter-attack. He staggered under one particularly ruthless blow, and she swept with her left leg, sending him falling back out of the circle. The crowd's roar vibrated the stage beneath Dralen's feet, and he felt the buzzing of Jaela's girl fans in his bones.

He watched through tears as The Broom re-entered the ring, the hate in his face replaced by resignation. Jaela deflected his attempts to retake control of the tempo, and she finished him off with a foot pin sweep. She didn't even take the free shot as he was falling, though she could have put a foot-shaped bruise on his torso if she'd chosen; the fight had gone out of him long before.

He accepted her hand this time, letting her help him up, and patted her on the back as the referee declared her the winner, setting off another set of roars from the crowd and a stampede for the betting windows. Jaela was on Dralen in an instant. Before he knew what was happening, she had picked him up and put him over her shoulder and was spinning him around and around, much to the delight of the crowd.

He held onto her for balance once she set him down, as the arena was still spinning a bit.

"You didn't think I could do it, did you?"

"I have to admit I had my doubts, but that didn't keep me from betting a thousand rabble on you."

"Where in the mountains deep did you get a thousand rabble, Dralen?" Georgi said in much too loud a voice.

Jaela picked her up, and fear flashed over Georgi's face for a moment until Jaela held her up and blew a big raspberry on her tummy, then cradled her in her arms like a baby.

"Let's not go blabbing about that to Mami and Papi, yeah?" she whispered. "And maybe I'll buy you something nice with my winnings."

Georgi nodded conspiratorially, touching her nose.

"You beat the hateful man!" Brin shrieked.

"Sweep sweep!" Teekee babbled.

"Well, you just paid for our trip down here, and then some!" Her father held up his coin purse, which was bulging. "Your mother didn't want me to bet—"

"I didn't want you to bet *all* our spring savings, but never you mind. Our Jaela did us proud. Who would have thought such a thing was possible?"

Dralen stepped back as Jaela sank into her family's embraces. He had several thousand rabble to collect from the betting office, and he had to pick up Jaela's winnings as well. They'd made a year's earnings in one day, and she'd only been at this for three months.

A person wearing a gray suit with light blue accents cut in the Fenylbyr style approached from the crowd, fishing a black card from their pocket.

"Are you Baby Bee's manager?"

Dralen stifled a laugh. "I guess I am. Dralen." He shook their tan, manicured hand as he accepted the card, thick paper, dyed black, with the words *The Gilded Veil* written in gold ink, and the image of a golden curtain.

"I expect you'll be heading to Fenylbyr next."

"The thought had occurred to us."

"I don't want to presume, but if you need a contact in the business there, I can help you get set up. I work with foot fighting, of course, but I wonder if your client might be inclined toward more...theatrical pursuits?"

Dralen couldn't hold his laughter in this time.

"Jaela's not an actress, and I'm sure she's not interested in burlesque if that's what you're thinking."

Their laugh was like the tinkling of a tiny, delightful bell.

"Nothing of the sort. There is a theater in Fenylbyr that combines foot fighting, dancing, and costumes into a sort of play. Your friend here has the attributes to be a star. I am sure of it. No pressure, of course."

They pointed toward the card.

"My name is Iri, and I represent the Gilded Veil, among other interests. But do look me up if you find yourself in Fenylbyr looking to break into the business. I'd be more than happy to help get you set up."

"Much obliged."

Iri tipped their hat, gave a slight bow, and was gone.

Dralen tapped the card against his palm, then pocketed it as Jaela skipped over and slipped her arm into his.

"Want to come to dinner with me and my family?"

"Sure, why not?"

"And afterward, you can tell me what that suit was talking to you about, and what's on that card you just slipped into your pocket."

"What if I told you we might be taking another trip west following a mysterious stranger?"

Jaela's eyes grew bright, and she kissed him on the cheek, then squeezed his arm tightly and turned him toward the betting window.

"Let's go pick up our winnings, then see what else the world has in store for us."

ALSO BY DANI FINN

The Maer Cycle (*Hollow Road, The Archive,* and *The Place Below*), a classic fantasy trilogy with LGBTQ characters. It tells the story of the encounter between humans and the legendary hairy humanoids called the Maer and the struggle for the two peoples to reconcile their history and their future.

The Weirdwater Confluence duology (*The Living Waters* and *The Isle of a Thousand Worlds*) are a pair of romantic fantasy books with meditation magic. They are independent of the trilogy, but there are little connections. Both books are sword-free and death-free, in sharp contrast to the Maer Cycle. *Unpainted* is a standalone arranged marriage fantasy romance set in the same universe.

The Time Before series: *The Delve, Jagged Shard, Wings so Soft,* and *Cloti's Song,* a group of linked romantic fantasy standalones set 2,000 years before the Maer Cycle. Meant to be read before or after the other books, they tell the story of the fall of the great Maer civilization of old.

Stay tuned via my spam-free newsletter and find all my links and other info at https://linktr.ee/danifinn

Acknowledgements

This book I wrote and edited like a hermit in a cave. No one but me has seen the manuscript. If it's the worse for that, so be it. This one is personal. I made the cover myself, based on a photo of a stump I took in Switzerland, which inspired this story. I'm sure none of it's perfect, but it's all me.

That said, I never really write alone. Big shout out to the Anti-Weasel Crew: Connor, Krystle, Fiona, and Alistair, who helped keep me on track in drafting and let me bounce ideas off their brilliant brains. And an even bigger shout out to my kids, Fitz and Basti, who let me read it aloud to them in the final proofreading stage. This is the first book of mine they've read (most are wildly inappropriate for teenagers), and their enthusiasm was heartwarming, as were the funny looks they gave me whenever Dralen and Jaela started cussing at each other.

Thank you, gentle reader, for taking the time to read this little tale. I couldn't have done it without you.

About the Author

Dani Finn (they/them) is a nonbinary fantasy romance author who occasionally writes fantasy without romance as well.

They favor high-steam love stories that crisscross the gender spectrum, from swords and sorcery to sword-free fantasy with meditation magic and everything in between.

Printed in Great Britain
by Amazon